IGUANA
BOY

LIKE EVERYTHING ELSE I DO,
THIS IS FOR JENNIE AND ZAC.
J.B.

SAVES THE WORLD WITH A TRIPLE CHEESE PIZZA

JAMES BISHOP
AND ILLUSTRATED BY RIKIN PAREKH

HODDER CHILDREN'S BOOKS
FIRST PUBLISHED IN GREAT BRITAIN IN 2018 BY HODDER AND STOUGHTON
1 3 5 7 9 10 8 6 4 2

A CIP CATALOGUE RECORD FOR THIS BOOK IS AVAILABLE FROM THE BRITISH LIBRARY.

ISBN 978 1 444 93934 7

PRINTED AND BOUND IN GREAT BRITAIN BY
CLAYS LTD, ST IVES PLC

THE PAPER AND BOARD USED IN THIS BOOK ARE MADE FROM WOOD FROM RESPONSIBLE SOURCES.

HODDER CHILDREN'S BOOKS
AN IMPRINT OF
HACHETTE CHILDREN'S GROUP
PART OF HODDER AND STOUGHTON
CARMELITE HOUSE
50 VICTORIA EMBANKMENT
LONDON EC4Y 0DZ

AN HACHETTE UK COMPANY
WWW.HACHETTE.CO.UK

WWW.HACHETTECHILDRENS.CO.UK

CONTENTS PAGE

PROLOGUE

EVERYDAY SOMEONE, SOMEWHERE IS SAVED BY A SUPERHERO.

Imagine this:

A girl swept away by the current, stranded at sea in a rubber dingy.

SAVED BY A SUPERHERO.

A boy falling headfirst off a garage roof whilst trying to retrieve his frisbee.

SAVED BY A SUPERHERO.

A group of kids playing hide and seek. One is so good at hiding that all the others give up trying to find him, leaving him stuck halfway down the chimney of his own house.

SAVED BY A SUPERHERO.

A cat stuck in a tree, too afraid to climb back down.

NOT **SAVED BY A SUPERHERO.**

Superheroes don't have time for such nonsense.

However, a young boy stuck in a tree trying to save his pet cat?

SAVED BY A SUPERHERO.

Not the cat, though. Superheroes have much more important things to be doing, like saving people from burning buildings and, well, other boys stuck in trees.

A young boy stuck ... Wait ... It's the same tree.

OK, **SAVED BY A SUPERHERO,** but this is the LAST time. And, no, superheroes don't have time to save cats ... Where is that boy going? Don't climb back up there ...! Fine ... get yourself stuck. No one will save you this time.

A young boy stuck in a tree.

NOT **SAVED BY A SUPERHERO.**

Not this time.

Don't feel sorry for him. He had plenty of warning.

Oh great, here come the waterworks ...

That's NOT going to work.

You are not getting saved.

OK, FINE!

SAVED BY A SUPERHERO (as is the stupid cat).

Yes, every day, someone, somewhere, is saved by a superhero (and, sometimes, so is their stupid cat). But who are these superheroes? How did they become 'super' and, perhaps most importantly, how come all superheroes are kids?

Any kid could be a superhero. Your brother, your sister, the kid who sits next to you at school, even your best friend.

Surely not my best friend, you are thinking. We share everything together. *Right?* But it could be them – some kids go through their entire life never even knowing they have a superpower, or keeping it a secret, if they do.

Not all powers are immediately obvious. If one day you can suddenly fly, you are going to notice, but if your power is being able to accurately guess what colour sweet you are going to pick next out of a pick'n'mix bag … Well, that's not so obvious at all.

How a superhero comes to be is something of a mystery. Tests carried out have concluded it doesn't run in the family, it's not given away on the back of a cereal packet, or caused by freak accidents with radioactive waste. In fact, it's not caused by radioactive waste at all. So don't go drinking glasses of thick, green, oozy gunk in the hope you will be able to climb up walls, or turn invisible. You will just be very, *very* ill.

Superpowers are not something you gain through practice: throwing yourself repeatedly off a garage roof won't help you fly, let me tell you, and staring at a wall for hours on end won't allow you to suddenly see through it, (although it might make you hallucinate, and that hallucination might involve seeing through the wall, but that is purely your imagination, and not the emergence of a superpower).

There is a theory, and it's only a theory, that those who desperately wish to become superheroes, become superheroes. If there is nothing your heart desires more, then it will be your destiny.

What kind of powers you get landed with ... well, everyone chalks that up to sheer, dumb luck.

DYLAN

Dylan Spencer sat on his bed, doing what he did best: DREAMING of becoming a superhero. He was royally fed up of waiting. Dylan had just turned nine, but he had dreamed of being a superhero ever since he could remember. As a child, you're used to saying, 'When I grow up I want to be ...'

but, as all superheroes are in fact children, he didn't want to have to wait until he was older. He wanted to be a superhero right NOW, just like his brother and sister were.

Unlike his brother and sister, Dylan was a nice kid who often put other people's feelings ahead of his own. From a very early age he had felt a need to help others. The feeling had manifested in small ways: drying the dishes after his mum had done the washing-up, or helping his dad get rid of a wasp nest in their attic, by throwing his teddy bear at it. (Unsurprisingly, this hadn't helped and his dad had got covered in stings, stubbed his toe on an old record player and tripped over, but Dylan's intentions had been good.)

It was around the age of five that Dylan had learnt about the existence of superheroes.

'Superheroes like to help. Much like you, Dylan,' his mum had told him, when passing over a wet dish for him to dry.

'They also protect us from bad people, like that horrible Veggie Boy,' added Dylan's dad, who was sitting at the table looking at the news on his phone. 'But he's behind bars now, thanks to Metallic Kid,' he said, before explaining the legend of Metallic Kid ...

THERE WAS ONCE A SUPERVILLAIN CALLED: VEGGIE BOY
HA HA!
YOUR LEGS ARE NOW CARROTS, NO ONE CAN STOP ME!
UNTIL ONE DAY, HE CAME UP AGAINST A BRAVE SUPERHERO ...
STOP RIGHT THERE, VEGGIE BOY. YOUR DAYS OF TURNING PEOPLE INTO VEGETABLES ARE OVER!
VEGGIE BOY LAUGHED AND TURNED THE SUPERHERO'S HANDS INTO BROCCOLI,
TURNED HIS ARMS AND LEGS INTO PARSNIPS,
TURNED HIS FEET INTO AUBERGINES,
TURNED HIS BODY INTO A POTATO,

BUT LITTLE DID HE KNOW THAT *THIS* SUPERHERO HAD THE POWER TO TURN **VEGETABLES** INTO **METAL** ...

HE TURNED INTO A ROBOT, AND THE LEGEND OF **METALLIC KID** WAS BORN!

Metallic Kid was the very first superhero Dylan had heard about. After his dad had finished the story, Dylan knew what he wanted to do. He wanted to help people. He wanted to put bad, mean people behind bars.

He wanted to be a superhero.

Dylan was the youngest of the three Spencer children – the only one without powers. His sister, Millie, was fourteen and his brother, Sam, had recently turned sixteen. Both of them were a big deal in the Superhero Collective, the organisation you joined if you could prove yourself as a worthy superhero. The superheroes were based at a super-cool building known as 'Superhero HQ', which floated high above

the River Thames in London. It was where all of the superheroes came together to hang out and get assigned missions and stuff. Dylan had asked his brother and sister numerous times if they would take him to Superhero HQ one day, even just for a visit, but they had laughed in his face and walked away. At least they hadn't farted in his face, that would have been worse.

Sam, aka Arctic Thunder, had the ability to control the weather, creating hurricanes with his fingertips, while Millie Monday roasted chickens in thirty seconds, with her laser eye superpower, only active on a Monday. Luckily, she could also fly (but also only on a Monday). They both had such awesome powers and Dylan was beside himself with jealousy because they were always off, saving the world ...

SUPERHERO COLLECTIVE HQ ID PASS

NAME: MILLIE SPENCER

AKA: MILLIE MONDAY

SUPERPOWER: LASER EYES

AGE/HEIGHT: 14yrs/5ft

DISGUISE: HEADBAND/CAPE

FAVOURITE DAY OF THE WEEK: MONDAY!

SOMEWHERE, AT A FOOTBALL MATCH IN HEAVY RAIN ...
NO NEED TO THANK ME ...
AT
THANK YOU, ARCTIC THUNDER!
IT'S ALL IN A DAY'S WORK!

I DON'T HAVE TIME! STUPID CATS ...
BUT THEN ...
NO, SLEEPY DRIVER! THIS TORNADO WILL STOP YOU FROM CRASHING INTO THAT TREE!
THERE'S NO NEED TO THANK ME, IT'S ... OH WAIT, HE DIDN'T THANK ME. OH, WELL, IT'S ALL IN A DAY'S— ON THE OTHER HAND ...
YOU KNOW I JUST SAVED YOUR LIFE.
OH, REALLY?
YES. SO DO YOU HAVE ANYTHING TO SAY TO ME?
UH, SURE. THANK YOU, MR—
NO NEED TO THANK ME,
IT'S ALL IN A DAY'S WORK!

Dylan jumped off his bed and looked out of the window: sometimes he saw Sam, aka Arctic Thunder, flying around outside, leaving a trail of thunderclouds behind him. On Mondays, he would sometimes catch a glimpse of Millie, too. Dylan had to reluctantly admit that his brother, Arctic Thunder, truly was a great superhero. (Although it's worth pointing out he did have a habit of embellishing his stories. For example, as Dylan had heard many times before, Arctic's version of the stadium story somehow also contained fifty evil ninjas, the defusing of a nuclear bomb and overcoming a colony of mutant ants that fired acid from their antennae. All he had done, really, was change the weather ...)

While Sam really enjoyed superhero work, their sister Millie sometimes found it frustrating, only ever able to use her powers on a Monday. Too often, as chance had it, all the really cool superhero work happened on other days ...

MONDAY
WHAT'S WRONG, SIR?
ANYTHING I CAN HELP YOU WITH?
MY OVEN'S BROKEN AND I HAVE FORTY GUESTS INSIDE WAITING FOR THEIR CHICKEN DINNERS! WHAT AM I GOING TO DO?
THANK YOU, MILLIE MONDAY!
YOU SAVED THE DAY!

You would be surprised at the number of times Millie Monday bumped into a chef with a broken oven on a Monday. It happened A LOT.

So, yep, Dylan's brother and sister had everything he ever wanted. AWESOME superpowers. It wasn't really a surprise – they always seemed to have better stuff than Dylan, who had received hand-me-downs ever since he could remember. Nothing that he owned was new. Clothes, books – even his pet iguana had originally belonged to Sam, until he grew bored of it.

3 MONTHS AGO

'Hey, little bro, catch!' Sam said, and Dylan turned just in time to see an iguana hurtling through the air towards him. Dylan was a small kid, the smallest boy in his year, and

having an iguana thrown at him very much knocked him off balance. He hit the grass with a thud, his scruffy hair softening the blow.

Dylan was given no instructions from Sam, no idea as to how long he wanted Dylan to babysit his iguana for. That was three months ago and Sam hadn't mentioned his pet iguana since.

(BACK TO THE PRESENT ...)

'I wish I could save the world, Tumbler,' Dylan said, as he held the iguana up to his nose. 'Even just once, like Sam gets to do every single day.' (He had called the iguana Tumbler after the way it had flown through the air that day.) He'd asked what

Sam had called him, but just got a fart as a response. The worst kind – a smelly, fuzzy wuzzler.

'My brother and sister both have such awesome powers. Hopefully, one day, I will, too. Sam is always so horrible. I would make a much better hero than him. Maybe my powers will come soon. What do you think, Tumbler?'

The iguana looked back at him blankly.

'No,' Dylan continued. 'I don't hold out much hope, either,' he said, picking up his favourite comic and placing Tumbler underneath his bed just in time, as a giant raincloud rapidly formed inside his bedroom and started to break – raining cats and dogs everywhere (actually, as this is a story about superheroes, this isn't the best phrase to use, as there are superheroes who do, in fact, have the ability to make cats and dogs fall from the sky – it's actually where the phrase comes from – but, to avoid confusion, it wasn't literally raining cats and dogs; it was just raining, well, boring old rain ...)

Anyway, his brother, Sam, aka Arctic Thunder, had a habit of doing this. He would send a raincloud into Dylan's room, and then put a mini hurricane next to the door so that Dylan couldn't get out. When Dylan was good and soaked, his sister Millie would enter and dry him off using her laser vision, so that their parents wouldn't find

out. This happened every single Monday.

'Please can I come out now?' asked Dylan, who had given up trying to read his comic, as it rapidly fell apart in his hands.

'Not until you say it,' said Millie, sniggering outside his bedroom door.

'But I've already said it a hundred times.'

'Then say it a hundred and one times,' added Sam, also sniggering.

'Do you really have nothing better to do than lock me in my room? If I was a superhero, I would be out in the world, helping people!'

'But you're not a superhero, and you never will be,' said Millie, snidely.

'Yeah, you don't have a power and, even

if you did, they would never invite you in to the Superhero Collective. They have certain standards and you simply don't meet them,' added Sam.

Dylan paused. Then he reluctantly said what his brother and sister wanted to hear (for what was actually the three hundredth time).

'My name is Dylan Spencer, I am nine years old, and I just wet the bed.' Despite the noise of the erupting hurricane and the pattering sound of falling rain (not cats and dogs falling, these noises are different: dogs make a terrible whining sound as they fall, while cats remain quiet, confident of landing on their feet), Dylan could hear his brother and

sister rolling around on the floor, laughing. He wasn't sure why they still found it so funny, having heard it over a hundred (three hundred) times. Eventually, the door opened. Millie dried Dylan and his room off with her laser eyes, leaving only one small wet patch in the centre of his mattress.

'It's very big of you to admit it, Dylan, but you really should have stopped wetting the bed by now,' said Sam.

Millie patted him on the back and laughed.

Then Sam's phone rang (playing 'Barbie Girl' by Aqua. He would hum along every time it went off and sing 'come on, Arcti, let's go party...')

Sam put his finger to his ear. This was how Superhero HQ communicated with the superheroes – with SUPER-COOL ear pieces:

'Absolutely, sir, I will be there right away. I'll let Millie know, too.' Sam touched his ear once more and turned to face his sister. 'That was Ron Strongman. We have to go – a rhino has escaped from Bristol Zoo and is running around causing mayhem.'

'Sounds pretty terrible,' replied Millie, coolly. She turned to her younger brother. 'I'll tell you what, Dylan. We'll head off and save the WORLD, and you can stay here and save your mattress – by changing the sheets.'

He could hear their laughter all the way down the stairs.

In that moment he was certain that one day, he would develop a power. And when he did, he would be better, stronger, and fiercer than both of them put together!

After he was sure that Sam and Millie had left the house to save the world from a rhino, Dylan headed outside to the garden to play with his cars (which had, of course, originally belonged to Sam). There were five in total: three only had two wheels; one was covered in paint; while the other was severely burnt (it had probably happened on a Monday).

He placed Tumbler in the sandpit nearby and set the cars up, ready to launch them off a small wooden ramp, made from the broken shed at the end of the garden. Dylan hadn't noticed that the ramp was facing in the direction of the sandpit, as he was too busy polishing his favourite cars, the Hyundai and the Hummer.

'Please welcome, for your entertainment, the amazing stunt-car driver, Dylan Spencer!' He grabbed hold of the burnt-out Hyundai car and pushed it towards the ramp. He let go and the car flew off the edge – straight onto the head of Tumbler.

'OUCH!'

Dylan froze.

'Hello?' he said.

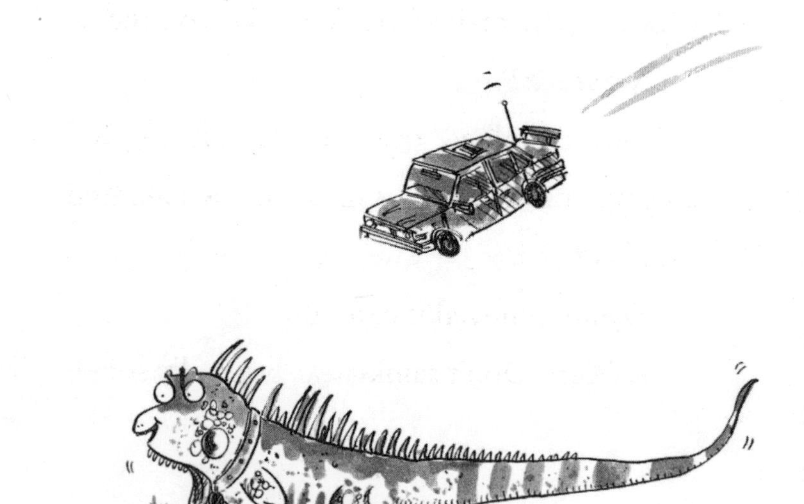

'Dude, that really hurt! Why did you throw a car at me?'

Dylan walked over to the pit to find Tumbler staring up at him, the car balanced on his head.

Dylan removed it carefully.

'Cheers. Don't think a car-hat really suited

me. I'm more of a flat-cap kinda guy.'

'You're talking!' Dylan exclaimed.

'I'm always talking, kid. It's you that's finally listening.'

'But you're an iguana.'

'I'm fully aware of that, thank you for clarifying. And now you can hear me, let me set one thing straight. My name is not Tumbler.'

'It's not?' Dylan sat down in front of him, still in shock.

'No. Tumbler? Duuuude – that's a terrible name for an iguana.'

'I'm sorry. I wasn't sure what Sam had called you.'

'Whoah, Sam had no right to choose my

name any more than you did. His was even worse by the way. "Spartacus"? That's an appalling name for an iguana. Then again, he came up with the name "Arctic Thunder" for himself, so what would you expect? Abysmal name for a superhero. No, if it were me, I would have called myself "The Blizzard Lizard".'

'I'm sorry. I didn't know. What shall I call you? Should I call you The Blizzard Lizard?'

'Nah, my name is Paul.'

'Really, Paul?' Dylan couldn't help but laugh.

'Yes, really,' replied Paul. 'Don't giggle, dude. Paul is a good, strong, solid iguana name. Lots of iguanas are called Paul, but I guess you'll find that out now you can speak to us.'

'Speak to you ...? Wait ...! You think I can speak to animals?' said Dylan, hopefully.

'Hmm, let's see ... Can you understand that cat?'

Dylan walked over to the neighbours' cat, Whiskers, who was perched on the fence, staring at Paul. 'Hello, Whiskers, how've you been?'

Dylan turned back to face Paul. 'No, it just meowed at me,' he said.

'What about that bird sitting on that branch over there?'

'I can hear it whistling.'

'Thought so. Not animals, kid. Looks

like you can only speak to iguanas. Some superpower that is!'

Dylan spent the next hour talking to animals. More accurately, he spent the next hour talking *at* animals. The only animal to reply was Paul, the iguana.

The cat meowed, the next-door dog barked, the bird on the branch kept whistling, and a frog he found squatting on a lily pad in the pond completely ignored him.

Dylan had to face facts. He could only talk to iguanas. His superpower had finally come in, and it was most definitely not awesome.

DYLAN'S NEW SUPERPOWER

For most superheroes, the first few days of exploring their newly discovered power are full of excitement and wonder. Inevitably there are a few scraped knees, banged heads and burnt chickens, but that's to be expected as they come to grips with their WICKED-COOL new abilities. They also can't wait to

tell everyone exactly what they can do.

Dylan, on the other hand, spent his first few evenings after school in an old tent at the bottom of the garden, talking to Paul. He told no one, not even his parents or his friends at school, but especially not his brother and sister, who would have probably rolled around on the floor, laughing until they wet themselves. Wait, maybe he *should* tell them ...

Precisely what he *didn't* want was to be able to understand iguanas. Yes, Dylan reckoned he might just have the WORST SUPERPOWER EVER! How could he use his power to help others? The only thing he could think of was if someone wanted to buy an iguana, he could go to the shop with them to ask the iguana if it was fully toilet trained … but that wasn't exactly saving the world, only someone's sofa.

It was the story of Metallic Kid that gave Dylan hope. When Metallic Kid had first found out his power was turning vegetables into metal, he must have thought there was very little use for it beyond a good practical joke when someone was biting into a veggie burger. But now he was a robot. A living, breathing (actually, maybe not breathing …) robot.

And Metallic Kid wasn't the only superhero who, on the surface of things, had a pretty terrible power but somehow made it work. Just look at Terrifying Suzanne …

YOU CAN'T DRAW ON WALLS! WASH IT OFF, YOU FOOLS!

I DON'T HAVE TIME TO HELP YOU GET THAT STUPID CAT OUT OF THAT TREE!
EEK!

So, Dylan spent quite a few days at the bottom of the garden with his new friend, trying to figure out how best to use his newly discovered (terrible) power.

Paul was certainly an interesting iguana. Definitely the most interesting one Dylan had spoken to, EVER. (Of course, he was the only iguana Dylan had spoken to, EVER, but nonetheless Paul took it as a huge compliment.) Sometimes Paul would be so ecstatic he was talking to a human, he would perform a salsa dance, purely for Dylan's entertainment. Dylan would rather he was watching *Strictly*.

Dylan discovered that Paul was two years old – which roughly translated into human years as two years old, according to Paul. Dylan tried to explain to Paul that dog years were seven times longer than human years, but this only confused Paul, who was convinced that if all dogs aged seven times faster than humans, they must also be able to time travel. Then, Paul stood on his back legs, raised his arm in the air, shouted, "To infinity and beyond!" and barked like a dog.

Despite the odd disagreement, Dylan and Paul discovered they had a lot in common. For example, their favourite colour was green. Dylan had always admired Paul's green skin and could now tell him. Paul, again, took this as a huge compliment, bowing profusely. They both loved climbing trees, and they could both touch the tip of their nose with their tongue. (Paul could actually reach considerably further, but he didn't want to show off too much.)

Dylan and Paul both shared the same taste in lemonade branding. Their favourite was Tesco own-brand – just the right amount of fizz. Dylan enjoyed feeding lemonade to Paul, just as he was falling asleep, so Paul would wake up again, pretty hyper, and they could carry on chatting into the night.

Both Dylan and Paul had moved from their first homes at an early age. Dylan had originally lived in a place called Wales. Paul thought Dylan was lying as he knew that whales lived in water, and if Dylan had been born in the sea, his skin would have

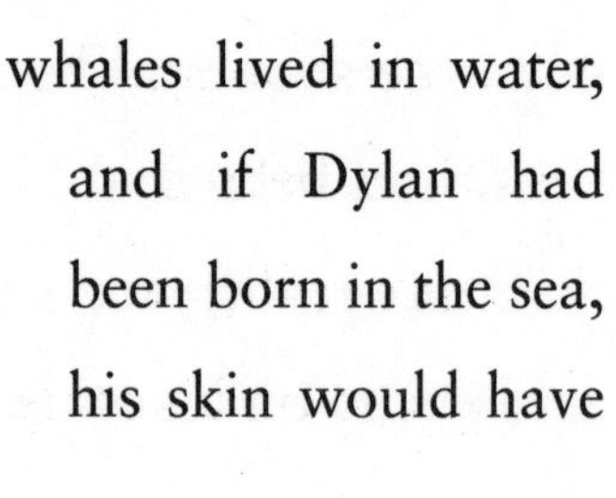

been all wrinkly and saggy (like Paul's). Added to this, Dylan couldn't actually remember Wales, but he had his parents to remind him of where he had come from. It was a place called Swansea.

Swans and whales? He's definitely making it up, thought Paul.

Paul, however, had no one to tell him where he was born. His earliest memory was living in a pet shop with some of his closest friends. Then, four months ago (both in human and iguana months), Sam had come in to the shop and bought Paul, leaving all the others behind.

'That's really sad,' said Dylan, patting his new friend on his scaly back.

'I miss them a lot. They were a great bunch. And pretty heroic ...' said Paul, the essence of an idea suddenly beginning to form in his mind.

'Heroic?' said Dylan, the essence of an idea forming in his mind, too.

'Oh, yeah. Brave, strong, incredibly intelligent and fearsome ... Did I mention fearsome?'

'They are iguanas, like you, right?' said Dylan, not entirely convinced.

'Of course they're iguanas! The most heroic iguanas that ever lived! Sure would be great to see them again ...'

Heroic iguanas, thought Dylan. *Maybe they can help me reach my full potential.*

Maybe I can become a superhero after all ...

That night, as Dylan slept, surrounded by his superhero toy collection, he had the most vivid dream of his life. He was used to fantasising about becoming a superhero – after all, it was all he had ever wanted to be – but this dream was different. It felt real.

Before, in his dreams, he had been flying aimlessly over mountains, or being incredibly strong and picking up large objects and holding them above his head. This time, however, he dreamed he was a real-life superhero, using his power for the benefit of all mankind. (That, after all, is the true definition of a superhero.) In his dream, he was running through a dense and dark forest. He couldn't see the ground beneath him, so he had to place his feet almost by instinct to avoid tripping on the countless tree roots protruding from the uneven ground. Paul was anxiously clinging to his shoulder, his tail flailing in the air as they reached maximum speed.

'HE'S GAINING ON US!' shouted Paul.

'HANG ON ...! ALMOST THERE ...' screamed Dylan.

At this point they managed to break out of the dense forest into a vast and barren desert.

'I THINK WE LOST HIM ...' said Dylan, wiping

the sweat from his brow.

Suddenly, a large man appeared behind them. He was perhaps ten times the size of Dylan, and full of muscles. Even his muscles had muscles. In fact, his name was, simply, 'Muscles'.

'I HAVE TRAPPED YOU, DYLAN. ANY LAST WORDS?' the man boomed.

'SURE, HOW ABOUT A TALE?' replied Dylan, airily.

'NO STALLING. I AIN'T GOT TIME FOR A STORY ...'

'NOT THAT KIND OF TALE ...' replied Dylan, with a smile.

Just then, four iguanas appeared behind him. These were no ordinary iguanas: they were brave, strong, incredibly intelligent and fearsome (did I mention fearsome?) iguanas. One perfectly timed swoop of their tails, and Muscles found himself flying through the air before being knocked to the ground. The iguanas were dressed as ninjas and boasted all the moves of kung fu experts.

Once Muscles was on the ground, they karate-chopped and Chinese-burned him

until he couldn't get up again.

'YOU WIN ONCE MORE, DYLAN! I PROMISE I WILL NEVER ATTACK THE CITY AGAIN ...' yelped Muscles.

'THE CITY IS SAVED, THANKS TO ME!' shouted Dylan triumphantly.

But if Dylan had been feeling optimistic about his new power, he was in for a rude awakening ...

Dylan jumped out of bed, banging into his brother's backside for what must have been the hundredth time (it was the three-hundred and twenty-first time, if you're interested in that kind of thing).

Sam thought it was hilarious to use his powers to hover over his brother's bed and let out a little parp (fart, toot, trump, whiff, guff, bottom burp, whoopee, stinky flump, fuzzy wuzzler, beef pie, gut churner, eggy bum bomb, nasal destroyer or whatever it is you like to call a rotten air fizzler).

It was a rude awakening, indeed.

'That's not funny, Sam,' said Dylan, rubbing his head and holding his nose.

'Not to you, maybe, but it is to me!'

retorted his floating brother, with a hearty, superhero laugh. 'And, as a superhero, my opinion is more important than yours.'

'Yeah, well, maybe you're not the only superhero here,' said Dylan, before instantly regretting it.

Sam looked at Dylan in amazement and thumped down out of the air and onto Dylan's bed.

To look at them, you wouldn't have known they were related. Dylan was skinny and short, with a large volume of black, unruly hair. Sam was the complete opposite: muscular and tall, with neat, slicked back light brown hair.

'Have you finally got a ...?' said Sam,

looking eagerly at his brother.

Dylan tried to backtrack. 'No, I was, uh ... talking about Millie. She has powers, so I was talking about her.'

'But our sister isn't *here*. You said I wasn't the only superhero here. You have, haven't you? You have a superpower!'

'No, I don't!' said Dylan, desperate to drop the subject entirely.

'You do! Look! You've gone all red. Wait a second ... it's embarrassing, isn't it? Oh, this is brilliant, go on, what is it?'

'I'm not saying.'

'So you admit it! Good for you, buddy.' Sam took hold of Dylan by his shoulders and wrestled him into a headlock. He then formed a tiny raincloud over Dylan's head to make his hair all wet (just because he could).

'Let me guess ... your farts smell like flowers?'

'No, that's stupid.'

'Pretty useful if you let a fuzzy wuzzler loose on a school trip or something. OK, so it's not that.' Sam paused, and looked at his brother searchingly. 'Oooh, I know – you can grow your fingernails really quickly? You can scratch all the other superheroes' backs at HQ! No? OK, umm, maybe you can turn hair into spaghetti? With hair like yours, you would always have lunch with you wherever you went! Wait, I know, I bet you can breathe through your ears and hear through your nose!'

'I DON'T have a power!' said Dylan, forcing himself free from the headlock, before falling back heavily onto his rain-soaked mattress.

'OK, OK!' said Sam, 'I believe you. I'm just pulling your leg. I doubt you'll ever have a power, even a dumb one like being able to lick your elbow or turn your face green or something.'

'Thanks for the support, Sam, as always.'

'I'm not supporting you, Dylan – surely you must see that?'

'I was being sarcastic.'

(Sam may have been a superhero, but he wasn't super-quick on the uptake.)

'Ah, yes, I forgot you did that. Hey, maybe that's your power! Sarcastic Boy!'

Dylan took a deep breath. 'It's not the power that makes a hero super, it's what they do with it. And I will be a superhero, I know I will.'

Sam pointed his finger directly at Dylan's chest. 'Now, you listen to me, brother. It IS the power that makes a hero super, and don't you dare let anyone fill your head with nonsense that it's not. There is no room at Superhero HQ for people with stupid, useless powers! We need strong heroes with real powers who can help save the world. That will never be you.'

Sam opened the door and went to leave,

but at the last moment he turned back to face Dylan. 'And if you do have a power, don't even think for a second about becoming a supervillain, because I will take you down in a heartbeat. Actually, maybe you should be a supervillain, someone like you would be easy to take down. In fact,' – and here Sam smiled evilly – 'if you do become a villain, we'll just wait until a Monday and Millie can deal with you. Taking you down would be as much a waste of my time as saving a cat from a tree.'

And with that, Sam left the room.

Dylan had managed to keep his power a secret for now, but he knew it wouldn't be long before someone figured it out. He reached down and grabbed Paul from underneath his bed. He was still hiding from the smell Sam had left lingering.

'Hey, dude, got any of the fizzy stuff?' Paul licked his lips in anticipation.

'I'll fetch you some lemonade as soon as we've been to the pet shop, Paul.'

Because Dylan wasn't going to be defeated easily. *I'm gonna get me some kung fu iguanas*, he thought.

The shop where Paul had been bought by Sam was called Pets Behaving Badly. It was at the end of Dylan's street, less than a five-minute walk away from his house.

Paul crawled into Dylan's backpack and they entered. Inside, the shop was dark and dirty. And it smelled. It smelled really bad.

Think of something really smelly, add a couple of your granddad's dirty old socks, your baby sister's full nappy, some mouldy cheese, a few buckets of elephant poo, a jar of eggy bum bombs, and the hair of your dog after it's been swimming, then give it a big stir with a (used) toilet brush. That was pretty much the smell.

The man behind the counter wore thick, black-framed glasses and had a big, bushy beard. 'Welcome to Pets Behaving Badly, where you will find the naughtiest pets at the nicest prices!' he said, with a grin. Next to him sat a boxer dog, who was seated on his own swivel-chair.

'Naughty pets? I don't understand,' said Dylan, looking around the shop. All the cages had thick metal bars, and it was hard to see inside them as the shop was also very dark. 'Wait. Is that dog chewing gum?'

'Yep. I try to take it away from him but he

just snarls at me until I give it back. He is a very naughty dog.'

At that moment, Paul sneaked out of Dylan's backpack, and took up his prime position, on Dylan's shoulder.

The shopkeeper took one look at the iguana and fell backwards off his chair, screaming, 'Where did you ...? How did you ...? Why did you bring him back?'

'Ah,' said Paul (although only Dylan could hear him). 'I should have pointed out that I have a bit of a bad reputation here.'

'You don't say,' said Dylan, peeking around the counter to see the shopkeeper huddled in a ball.

The dog clearly recognised Paul, too, as he

was now hiding under a blanket.

'I'm looking for a friend for my iguana, Paul. I think he might be a little lonely. Do you still sell iguanas?'

The shopkeeper was now under the blanket with the dog. 'At the very back, in the "Untameable" section,' came the muffled reply. 'Take any iguana you want. You don't have to pay. Take them all, if you like!'

Dylan made his way to the Untameable section. There was one solitary cage. Inside were three rather sweet-looking iguanas.

'Guess who's back, guys!' said Paul, standing on his back legs, raising both his front legs in the air above his head.

'Paul?' said one of the iguanas.

'It can't be,' said another. 'It is! He came back for us!'

'I told you I'd be back. I'd never leave an iguana behind,' said Paul.

'Who's the meat bag?' said another iguana, looking directly at Dylan. The iguana had one normal sized eye and one big red eye.

'I'm no meat bag!' said Dylan, indignantly. 'My name is Dylan Spencer and I can speak to iguanas!'

'Only iguanas,' added Paul, helpfully.

A moment went by as the three iguanas in the cage stared at Dylan. They then fell to the floor in fits of uncontrollable laughter.

'Only iguanas? HA! HA! HA!'

'What good is that?'

'Tough break, kid!'

'What should we call you ... Iguana Boy?'

The laughter continued for quite some time. The iguanas occasionally paused for breath or to shout 'Iguana Boy', which made them laugh even more. Dylan was not amused. When the laughter died down, Paul made the introductions.

'So, "Iguana Boy", I want you to meet my friends. On the left there is Paul.' He pointed to the iguana with the large, red eye.

'Wait, your name's Paul, too?' said Dylan.

'I told you it's a popular name for an iguana.'

'Good to meet you, kid. If it helps, people call me Crazy Red-Eye Paul, or just good old Red-Eye for short.'

'Why do they call

you *Crazy* Red-Eye Paul?' asked Dylan.

Without a moment's hesitation, Red-Eye ran as fast as he could at the side of the cage, head first. He hit his head on the bars with an almighty THUD, did a backflip and landed in the water bowl with his legs in the air.

'I see,' said Dylan.

'Oh, and you probably hadn't noticed, but I've got one big red eye.'

Dylan nodded, trying to keep his face neutral. Of course he had noticed. Everybody noticed.

'This guy right here is Paul,' said Paul, moving on to the next iguana.

'Another one?' Dylan smacked his hand to

his forehead in disbelief.

'It's a popular name for an iguana,' said all the Pauls, at the same time.

'They call me Smelly Paul, because, truth be told, I smell like an old can of mouldy beans which has been left out for hours on a hot summer's day, mixed with the breath of a dog who has eaten nothing but tuna for a week

and not brushed his teeth.'

'That's an incredibly detailed description,' said normal Paul. 'I mean, it's accurate, but, far too detailed. Anyway, last but not least, to your right is—'

'Let me guess, Paul. Nice to meet you, Paul,' said Dylan, sticking out his hand.

'HOW DARE YOU? My name is not Paul, and I have quite honestly never been so offended in my entire life!'

'I'm s-so sorry, I didn't th-think …' stuttered Dylan.

'No, you most certainly did not, Iguana Boy.'

'What is your name, if I may ask?'

'My name is Pauline,' said Pauline, who folded her arms, turned away from Dylan and huffed dramatically.

There was another short, awkward pause, and then Paul said: 'That's the introductions sorted – now, how about we break you out of here and head home?'

'Wait a second,' said Dylan, slowly moving backwards from the cage. 'When the shopkeeper saw you, he fell over backwards and hid under a blanket. In fact, so did his dog. He also said I could take any iguana I liked from the "Untameable" zone of this pet shop – a pet shop that is exclusively for naughty animals.'

'What's your point?' said Crazy Red-Eye Paul, who had managed to remove himself from the water bowl, and was now chewing on his own leg.

'My point is,' said Dylan slowly, 'why are the shopkeeper and his dog so afraid of you – why does he think you are untameable?'

This, if you think about it, was a very reasonable question to ask, given the circumstances. Dylan had thought getting to know a few extra iguanas (that were possibly kung fu experts) might come in handy in his quest to become a superhero, but he also didn't want a group of unruly, untameable reptiles running wild around his house. Especially if they weren't toilet trained.

'Why is he scared of us? Who wouldn't be scared of four kung fu experts that don't know the meaning of danger?' said Paul, waving his front legs above his head again, before crouching down and leaping into the air.

'Four weapon specialists who can make swords and nunchucks out of sawdust and a toilet roll?' continued Pauline.

'Four secret agents who single-handedly stopped the crown jewels from being stolen just by being super-awesome and stuff,' added Smelly Paul.

'And did Paul mention that we're VAMPIRES?' said Crazy Red-Eye Paul, who was casually leaning against the back of the cage, picking his teeth with the tip of his tail.

The other iguanas turned around to face him at the same time. They didn't look too happy.

'What?' said Red-Eye, unsure why everyone was looking at him.

'I don't believe a single word of any of your stories,' said Dylan.

'Why would we lie?' replied Paul.

'Can you prove any of these claims?' asked Dylan.

Without a moment's hesitation, Red-Eye bit Smelly Paul on the neck.

'OW! What was that for?'

'He said prove it, and we're vampires, remember?' said Red-Eye, enthusiastically.

'Let me stop you there,' said Dylan, pulling open the cage door. 'I may not believe you, but I'll admit you're pretty inventive. Maybe that inventiveness will come in handy in my mission to become the greatest superhero EVER. Besides – and I can't believe I'm saying this – but any friend of Paul's is a friend of mine.'

Dylan opened the cage to free the iguanas, and the Pauls and Pauline climbed onto his shoulders and joined the original Paul.

Dylan made his way back across the pet shop towards the door. The shopkeeper saw them coming and ran into one of the larger, (luckily) empty cages nearest the entrance, closing the door firmly behind him.

'Please, don't ever bring them back. I beg you.'

The shopkeeper looked truly terrified. Dylan glanced down at the iguanas again. He couldn't imagine them as kung fu experts, secret agents or athletes. Maybe they really were vampires ... but that was even more ridiculous. They were pretty normal looking.

But, as he left, Dylan found new hope. If the iguanas could strike this much fear into a large man and a big dog who owned his own swivel-chair, maybe his superpower really was awesome after all. Maybe this was the moment he had always been waiting for ... maybe Dylan was about to become a superhero!

THE PLATYPUS KID

Meanwhile, on the other side of town, there was somebody who had NEVER wanted to become a superhero. *Who wouldn't want to be a superhero?* you're probably thinking – flying around town, stopping criminals in their tracks (and ignoring cats in trees) ...

Celina Shufflebottom was born to be bad.

Ever since she was a little girl, all she had ever been good at was being bad. If you were waiting in line at the ice-cream van, you can bet Celina would be there to push in ahead of you. If you were blowing the biggest bubble of chewing gum the world had ever seen, Celina would be right there, ready to pop it …

Her parents were nice enough people, and all her friends at school were well behaved – at a glance Celina seemed to fit right in. But if you were to look a little closer, it was obvious something wasn't quite right.

It all stemmed from a deep hatred of being told what to do. Even the simplest of commands, like her parents asking her to put her toys away, her teacher setting her homework, or her friends asking her to hold one end of a skipping rope, filled her with an uncontrollable anger.

It didn't matter if it was something she wanted to do, or even something she was just about to do, like get in the bath her mum had just run, anger would consume her. Her freckled cheeks would turn fiery red. Her teeth would grind together, causing sparks as her upper and lower braces mashed against each other. She would wrap her fingers around her long red hair, pulling frantically until she could no longer bear the pain, no longer hold in the scream – which would escape from her mouth in seven simple words:

'NO ONE TELLS ME WHAT TO DO!'

Then, Celina would do her very best to do the exact opposite of whatever she had been told to do.

Like, one time Dylan had felt sorry for Celina – she was new in school – so he decided to sit next to her during art class. Celina was drawing a zoo with lots of different animals. 'That's a really cool picture,' Dylan said.

'Thank you, I've been practising it for ages,' said Celina.

'Here's mine,' said Dylan, showing Celina his picture of a zebra that looked like a cat with a hippo on it. 'Ah, I'm so bad at drawing,' he said with a sigh.

'Can you draw lions?' asked Dylan.

'Obviously,' replied Celina, coolly.

'You should totally add one to your zoo picture,' suggested Dylan.

'NOBODY TELLS ME WHAT TO DO!' exclaimed Celina, storming out of the classroom in a fit of rage.

That was the first and only time Dylan Spencer told Celina Shufflebottom what to do, or even made a suggestion. Over the next few hours, he noticed she didn't take being told what to do very well at all. She would actually go out of her way to do the exact opposite on some occasions.

Celina soon realised the only way she could ever be happy was if no one told her what to do. Not her parents, teachers, friends, that stupid kid Dylan who had been trying to be her friend, not even the queen, not anyone, not ever again. This is why she wanted to rule the world. This is why Celina Shufflebottom secretly dropped out of Year 5 at Dylan's school to be the world's most EVIL supervillain ... and Dylan never saw her again.

If there was a cat stuck up a tree ... well, Celina had most likely put it up there herself. Not because she didn't like cats (she actually loved all animals – platypuses were her favourite), but because she knew it was the one thing that annoyed superheroes the most because they were expected to save them.

She would often write down a list of things that she thought would annoy superheroes the most:

1. SUPERVILLAINS TRYING TO TAKE OVER THE WORLD
2. CATS STUCK IN TREES

Little did she know, this list was actually pretty accurate. Something very similar had been scribbled on the wall of one of the toilet cubicles at Superhero HQ. The only difference being was that there was a third item on the list in the toilet:

③ SUPERHEROES WHO CAN'T FLY BUT STILL INSIST ON WEARING A CAPE

You're probably wondering how someone decides between being a superhero and a supervillain. It's actually incredibly simple.

When they finally get their superpower, they will either think: *How can this power help me to help others?* or *How can this power help me?* At their core, superheroes are selfless, while supervillains … well, don't expect them to share a packet of crisps with you (even if they don't like the flavour, even if it's cheese and onion … it's the principle).

It's as simple as that.

Supervillains don't work particularly well with others, which is why they often live alone. They don't come together like superheroes and meet up socially all the time for fun. There is no supervillain HQ; instead, they tend to live in vast, often dark and dingy 'lairs'.

Celina's lair was right in the heart of the city of London, and bucked the tradition of being dark and dingy. It was actually a light, airy and rather pleasant warehouse on the south side of the River Thames – she had been told by a supervillain she once met to find herself a dark and dingy lair, but she had decided against it, for her own perfectly reasonable reason of: NO ONE TELLS ME WHAT TO DO!

Although it looked fairly pleasant inside, it was far from it. Celina's warehouse could turn into the most secure and sophisticated prison in the world at the touch of a button. Innocent on the outside, terrifying on the inside. Just like Celina.

You might be wondering how a nine-year-old girl had access to a huge supervillain warehouse. (If not, you really should be. It is a little odd. Unless you were thinking about what you might be having for dinner tonight. What are you having? It's easy to get distracted. Actually, the word 'distraction' has an incredibly interesting origin story ...

Oh. Sorry. See, it's very easy to get distracted. Back to the story ...)

Celina's parents were estate agents, specialising in large industrial buildings in London. So all it took was for Celina to grab the keys to one of the many properties they managed and she had herself a fantastic new lair. Luckily, she chose a building only a few minutes' walk along the river, which she could access via the gate at the end of her parents' garden.

She would sneak out every night to sit down with her supervillain council and discuss the many ways she could take over the world.

'Welcome to the three-hundred and forty-seventh World Domination meeting, hosted by me, Celina Shufflebottom. Item one on the agenda this evening is, once again, how can I take over the world? Ideas please,' she said, looking around the table at her supervillain council.

At this point it's probably worth mentioning that Celina had a pretty special and rather distinct supervillain council. They were platypuses. (For those of you unaware of what a platypus is, it's basically a beaver with a duck's beak.)

In the world of supervillains, Celina was known as the Platypus Kid. She had discovered her power on a visit to Bristol Zoo a few years before, when a platypus, rather unexpectedly, had asked her for the time, wanting to know how long it would be until dinner.

She had spent the next hour running around the zoo trying to talk to lions, gorillas, leopards – even giraffes – but none of them had answered her. She had returned to the platypus enclosure feeling rather disappointed.

Since then, Celina had broken hundreds, perhaps even thousands, of platypuses out

of zoos across the world to build an army. The originals from Bristol Zoo now acted as her advisors on her supervillain council.

'Ideas, guys, come on!' said the Platypus Kid, banging her fist fiercely on the long mahogany table around which her supervillain council was seated.

After a moment of silence, a rather timid-looking platypus spoke.

'You could take all the world leaders hostage until they sign over control of their countries to you.'

Celina shot the idea down immediately. 'That won't work – one of the superheroes will just turn up and rescue them.'

'You could steal all the world's water, then

start a HUGE fire that would engulf the entire planet.'

The Platypus Kid hummed thoughtfully and looked up at the ceiling in contemplation.

'Yeah, totally!' said another platypus, sensing that this idea might be the one she finally went for, and wanting to claim some of the credit for himself. 'And then you could say you won't put it out until you're in charge of the world.'

'That's completely impossible,' Celina replied. 'Oceana Girl will turn herself into an entire ocean and she'll just put the fire out.'

The idea-hopping platypus shot the other platypus an evil glance, as if it was entirely his fault, and then folded his forelegs in a temper.

'You could maybe run for office, become prime minister, unite every country under the banner of world peace, and become the natural leader of the free world,' said another platypus, hopefully.

'Get out.' Celina pointed towards the door.

The platypus jumped off his seat and practically sprinted out of the door.

'Do we have the technology to turn everyone into monkeys?' asked a fifth platypus.

'No,' replied the Platypus Kid.

'Oh. Nothing from me then.'

'What about stealing all the money from

every bank in the world? You would be the richest person on the planet and could buy every single country!' tried another platypus, once again to no avail.

'I like it, but no doubt half the robberies will be stopped by another superhero! They ruin everything!'

The platypus that had been asked to leave was listening at the doorway. 'Then why not kidnap EVERY superhero. Without them, who would be able to stop you?' he said. He was desperately trying to win back Celina's approval so he could return to his seat and retrieve his sandwich box, which was underneath the table. 'Then all you would need to do is capture the world's leaders,

and get them to hand over all their power to you.'

'I've got it!' said the Platypus Kid, jumping from her seat. 'Why don't we kidnap every superhero? Then no one would be able to stop me!'

'Hey, that was my idea! I told you to do that.'

Celina whipped around to face the platypus skulking in the doorway. 'You told me to do that?

NO ONE TELLS ME WHAT TO DO!'

The Platypus Kid turned bright red and started to visibly shake with anger. She knocked everything on the table onto the floor with one violent sweep of her arm, then ran over to the platypus in the doorway. Dragging the platypus by the beak, she pulled him over to the table and threw him along it. The table was very slippery due to its polished surface – he slid down the whole length before crashing into the wall at the other end. Finally, the Platypus Kid grabbed his sandwich box, opened it up and ate the sandwich.

It was his favourite kind – peanut butter and sweetcorn – and the platypus began to cry (he was really hungry, after all).

Once the Platypus Kid had calmed down (after what seemed like about three years to the petrified platypuses), she set them all to work on her 'Superpower Neutraliser Machine'.

'Guys, get to work on the Superpower Neutraliser Machine,' she said.

It's a little-known fact about platypuses, but they are super, SUPER-intelligent. People often think that dolphins and monkeys are the closest in intelligence to humans and, in fairness, they are absolutely correct.

Here's a chart that proves it:

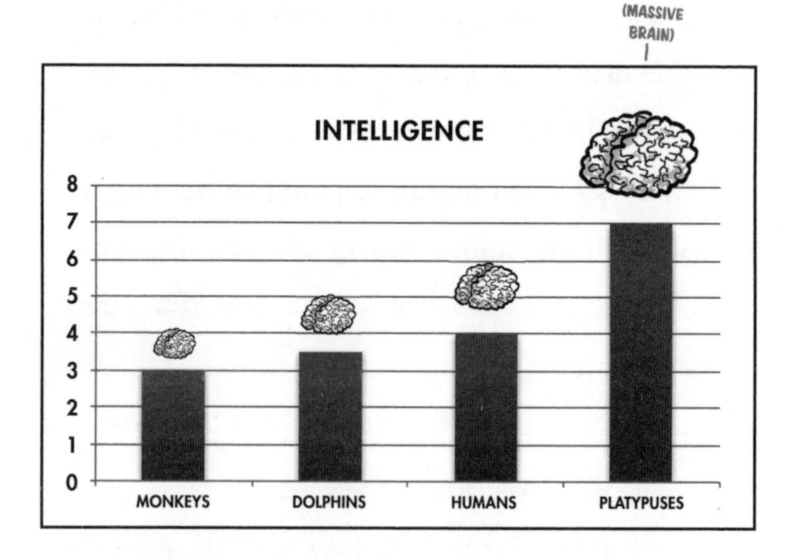

Platypuses are infinitely superior to humans. The majority of humanity's greatest inventions were, in fact, discovered by platypuses: electricity, the car, nuclear fusion, the telephone (the first word ever spoken across a phone line was actually a low growl. When Alexander Graham Bell came downstairs to find a fully functional phone in his living room he was surprised. Even more so when he saw a platypus holding a screwdriver standing over it). The list goes on and on. (However, it's worth noting that humans have invented some things, such as the spork, the yo-yo and, the best one of all, the selfie stick.)

At least if the platypuses could perfect the Superpower Neutraliser Machine, they reasoned, then the Platypus Kid would give them the credit and everyone would know how super-clever AWESOME they really were. If it worked, well, it would be more than easy to lock up every single superhero. And without superheroes, the world would be theirs for the taking ... or the Platypus Kid's, with her super-clever, AWESOME platypus sidekicks.

With the plan set in motion, all the Platypus Kid needed to do now was to set a trap. And get the attention of all the superheroes in the Superhero Collective.

'All I need now is to set a trap. And get the attention of all the superheroes in the Superhero Collective,' said the Platypus Kid to her supervillain council, before throwing back her head and releasing an evil laugh.

THE WORLD IN PERIL

They say that everyone remembers exactly where they were when big things happened to them. Dylan's mum would often recall where she was the day 'that' boy band (Dylan had forgotten the name) had broken up (she had been at the swimming pool with her friends, blaming her tears on the chlorine).

His dad remembered where he was when his beloved football team, Manchester United, had defeated Arsenal 8–2. (Dylan didn't really like football, but apparently this was a big deal.)

For Dylan, the moment he would never forget was the moment he first laid eyes on the Platypus Kid. He was sitting in his bedroom, desperately trying to think of a superhero name he could call himself that wasn't something stupid like 'Iguana Boy' (which is what his new friends the Pauls and Pauline insisted upon calling him).

All of a sudden, a flash of light and a low, static humming noise came from behind him. Dylan turned around to find the television had switched itself on. The screen showed a young girl wearing a bright yellow headband and matching eye mask. Something about the girl seemed vaguely familiar but her bright yellow headband was VERY distracting.

'RIGHT NOW, ALL THE TELEVISIONS IN THE WORLD ARE BROADCASTING MY EVERY WORD. I AM HERE TO TELL YOU THAT TONIGHT... ACTUALLY, WHILST I HAVE EVERYONE'S ATTENTION, I WOULD JUST LIKE TO SAY, FOR THE RECORD, THAT IT WAS NOT ME WHO LET OUT A ROTTEN AIR FIZZLER ON THE SCHOOL TRIP TO BATH CATHEDRAL. I STAND BY MY ORIGINAL STATEMENT THAT HE WHO SMELT IT DEALT IT ... ISN'T THAT RIGHT, JIM CAMPBELL?!'

She paused for breath.

'APOLOGIES, I'VE GONE OFF TRACK. WHERE WAS I? AH, YES, TONIGHT I WILL CAPTURE EVERY SUPERHERO ON THE PLANET AND LOCK THEM BEHIND BARS. THEN, I WILL TAKE OVER THE WORLD.'

The camera zoomed out to reveal a large warehouse containing a huge, empty prison cell. Behind the girl were hundreds of platypuses.

'MY NAME IS
THE PLATYPUS KID.
TOGETHER WITH MY ARMY OF PLATYPUSES, WE WILL RULE THE WORLD!
HA! HA! HA!'

She threw her head back in order to project her maniacal laugh as loudly as possible.

The screen went black and then cut to a news studio, with a rather confused-looking newsreader seated at his desk.

'I'm sorry about that interruption. It appears we are all doomed. Who could possibly stop a supervillain with a bunch of platypuses.' The newsreader paused. He then began laughing uncontrollably. Tears raced down his cheeks. 'Sorry … it's just so

ridiculous!' Here, he cleared his throat and took a moment to rearrange the papers on the desk in front of him, before continuing in a more serious tone: 'I understand that a press conference is being held at Superhero HQ in London. We're going live there, now, to listen to what Arctic Thunder has to say.'

Dylan watched the broadcast with growing despair as he listened to his brother speak: 'People of the world, don't worry. I mean, I doubt any of you are actually worried by a small girl who can talk to platypuses but, rest assured, we will stop her evil plans to "take over the world". I'm not exactly sure how she intends to "take over the world" with a bunch of platypuses. Maybe she'll ask them to peck us all until we surrender? HA! HA! HA! I mean, that's a TERRIBLE superpower. Being able to talk to a single, useless animal species! What an embarrassment! I know if I were related to someone with such a terrible superpower, I would die of embarrassment – or laughter, more likely! Anyway, I'm off to "save the world" from the *evil* Platypus Kid ...'

Arctic Thunder's laughter continued for a few moments until Dylan eventually turned the television off.

'I thought you had it bad, kid, only being able to talk to us, but that girl ... platypuses? That's a really tough break!' said Paul.

'He's laughing at her, but he might as well

be laughing at me.' Dylan sighed. 'When Sam finds out about my power, all he'll see is his stupid kid brother who can talk to a "single, useless animal species". No offence.'

'Actually, that is pretty offensive,' Pauline remarked, with a sniff.

'Yeah, we're not useless,' said Smelly Paul. 'We can change colour and blend into our surroundings.'

'That's chameleons,' said Paul, witheringly.

'Oh, yeah – chameleons are cool! Bet you wish you could speak to chameleons instead, don't you, kid?'

'I'm sorry, I didn't mean to offend you,' said Dylan. 'It's just I've wanted a superpower for so long. I wish I could show it off to Millie and Sam. But they will never think of me as a superhero!' Dylan flung himself back on the bed. 'I don't want to be a laughing stock!'

Pauline crawled up onto the bed next to Dylan. 'I feel for you, Iguana Boy, I really do,' she said, resting her tail on his shoulder.

'Truth be told, we've grown kinda fond of you. We don't want everyone laughing at you either,' said Paul.

Dylan sat up slowly. 'Thank you, guys. I really appreciate it.' He looked up and squared his shoulders. 'I'll go and make us a drink and then I have to know why that shopkeeper was so scared of you. And tell me the truth this time.'

Dylan went downstairs, feeling a little more

optimistic. Maybe, given the shopkeeper's reaction to the iguanas, his superpower really was secretly amazing.

In the kitchen he made some sweet cloudy lemonade, just the way the iguanas liked it. Five minutes later, as they politely sipped the fizzy drink through straws, the iguanas finally told him what had happened that one fateful day at the pet shop …

A MUM AND HER SON ARRIVE TO DROP OFF A CAGE OF IGUANAS, THE OWNER HAS POPPED TO THE TOILET SO THEY LEAVE.
Pets Behaving BADLY
MORE CUSTOMERS ARRIVE (OWNER IS STILL IN THE LOO) TO DROP OFF A RABBIT IN A BOX. THEY LEAVE IT NEXT TO THE IGUANA CAGE.
ON THE COUNTER NOW, MOLLY.
OK, OK, I'M DOING IT! THERE. HAPPY? I CAN'T HAVE ANYTHING FUN.
WHEN SNUFFLES JUMPED ON YOUR NAN WHILST SHE WAS ON THE TOILET, WAS THAT FUN?

ZZZZ
SNUFFLES CRASHES STRAIGHT THROUGH THE WINDOW, LEAVING BEHIND A HUGE MESS AND FOUR SWEET (IF GUILTY LOOKING) IGUANAS.
WE'RE FREE!

'It was carnage,' said Paul, remembering the day as if it were only last week. 'The shopkeeper thought we had done the damage, and was petrified of us. He kept calling us demons and thought we had risen from hell itself.'

'He even opened up that "Untameable" section just for us,' added Pauline.

'Snuffles was one crazy rabbit,' said Crazy Red-Eye Paul.

'Oh,' said Dylan.

'I still have nightmares about that rabbit,' said Smelly Paul.

'OK, so if I understand correctly,' continued Dylan, slowly, 'the shop owner was terrified because you destroyed his shop.

Only you didn't, a rabbit did.'

'That's it,' said Paul.

'A rabbit called ... Snuffles?' queried Dylan.

'Yep,' said Pauline.

'So that means you don't have some awesome power or hidden strength that can help me become the superhero I have always been destined to become?' added Dylan, a glimmer of hope still detectable in his voice.

'Yup,' the iguanas replied, looking down at the ground and avoiding eye contact.

'And, OK, I admit it, we're not vampires,' added Red-Eye.

'Then we're completely doomed!' cried Dylan, throwing himself onto his bed again and burying his head deep in his pillow.

He stayed in that position until he fell asleep. And when he slept, he dreamt that he was the BEST superhero EVER.

IT'S A TRAP

The Platypus Kid had been waiting impatiently for almost an hour. How long could it possibly take all the superheroes in the Superhero Collective to figure out her location? Her warehouse was actually less than a mile away from Superhero HQ as the crow flew (and most superheroes could fly

faster than crows). She hadn't done much to hide her location when she had broadcast her plans to the world – it was clearly a warehouse, and the river could be seen in the background.

Celina was starting to think the superheroes weren't taking her threat seriously. An hour had passed, and not a single superhero had arrived.

'I should have had the address written on my T-shirt, and put a fifty-foot neon sign above the building in the shape of a huge arrow. They're imbeciles!' she cried, exasperated.

'Grr,' replied one of her platypuses.

The Platypus Kid suddenly realised how

THE PLATYPUS KID'S SECRET LAIR,
WAREHOUSE,
RIVER THAMES,
LONDON

weird it was hearing a platypus growl. For so long she had been able to speak to them in human language, but at that precise moment, all she could hear was a disgruntled growl – just like anyone else would. Then she realised with delight why that might be … the Superpower Neutraliser Machine was WORKING!

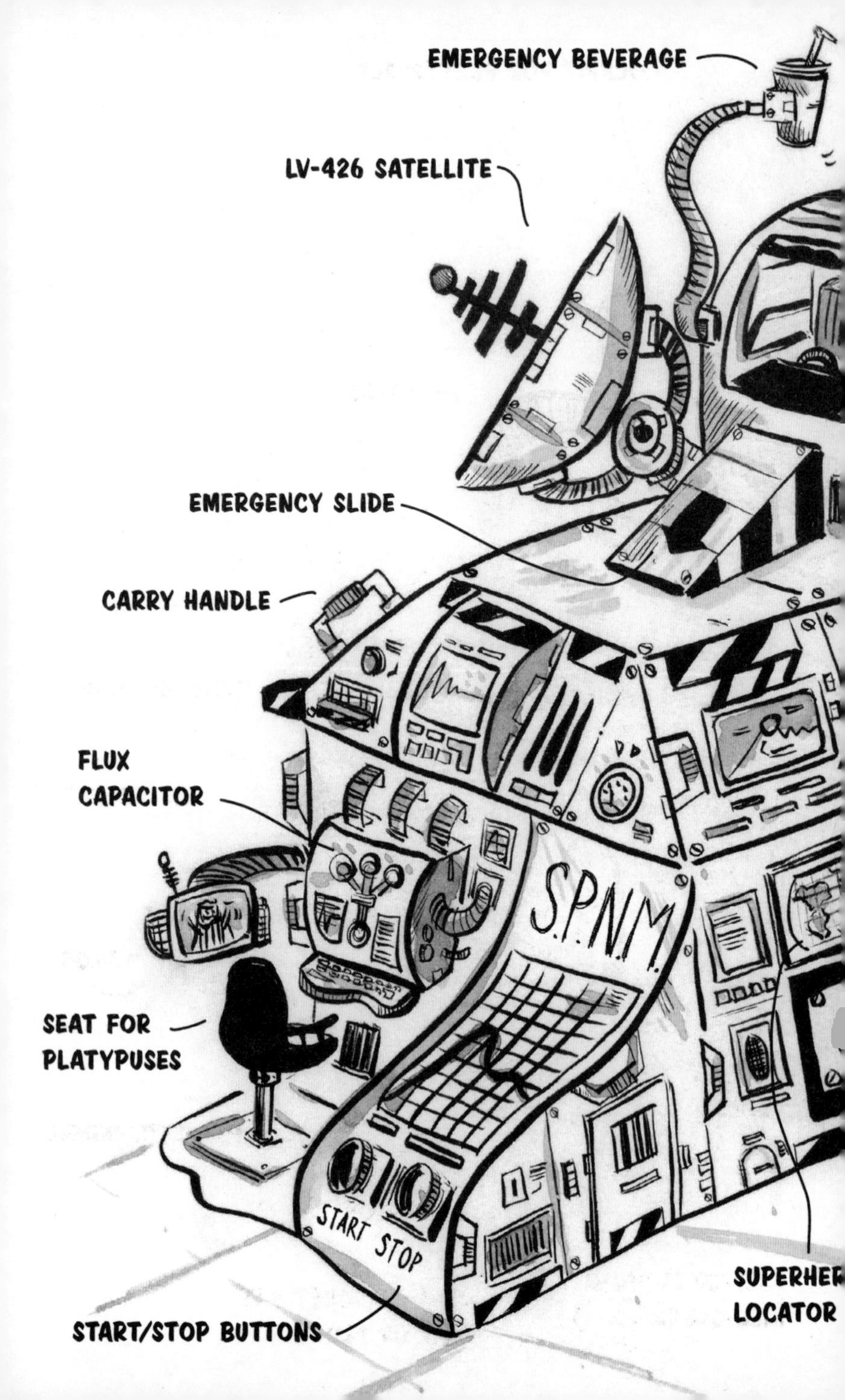
EMERGENCY BEVERAGE
LV-426 SATELLITE
EMERGENCY SLIDE
CARRY HANDLE
FLUX CAPACITOR
S.P.N.M.
SEAT FOR PLATYPUSES
START STOP
START/STOP BUTTONS
SUPERHER
LOCATOR

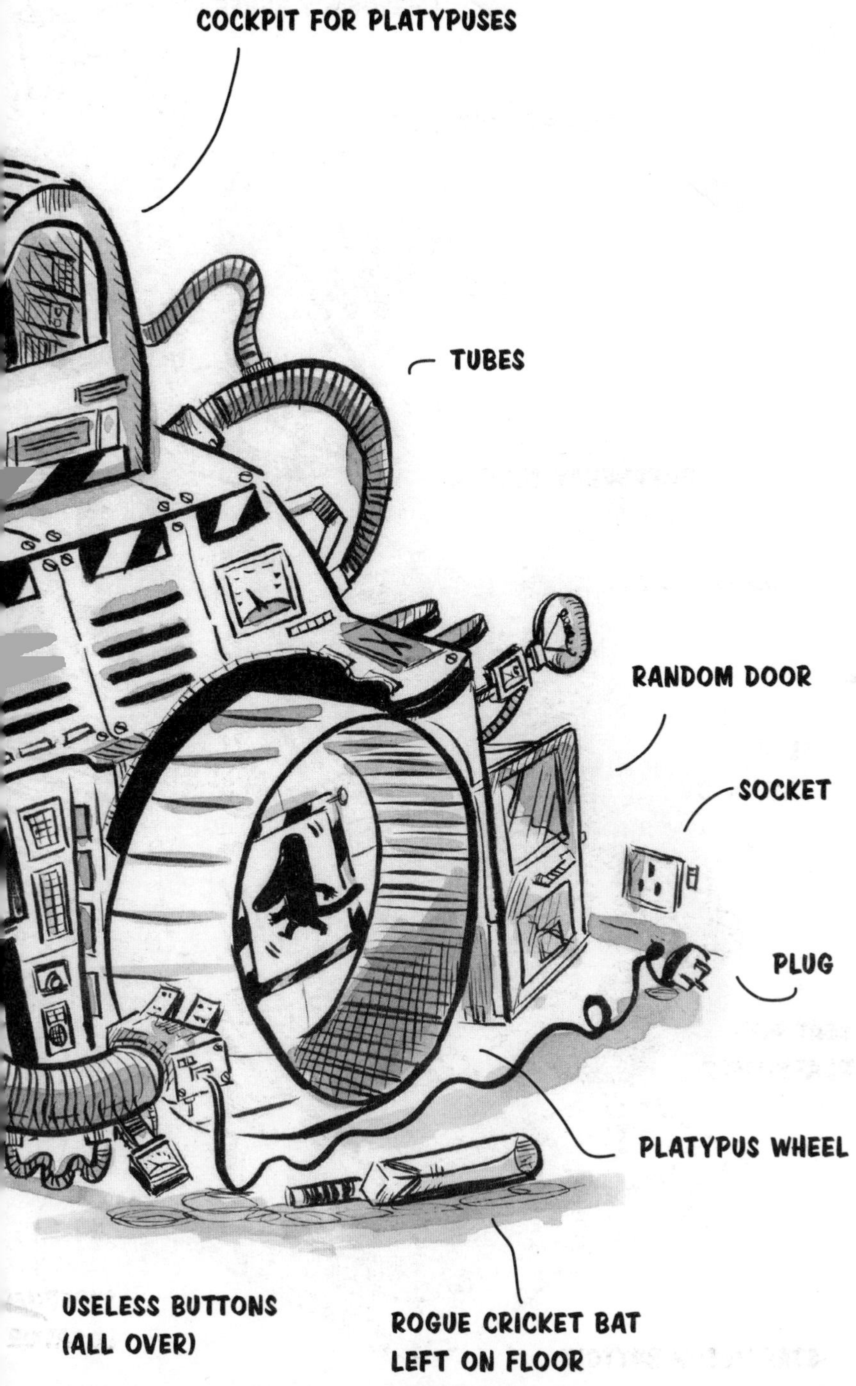

COCKPIT FOR PLATYPUSES

TUBES

RANDOM DOOR

SOCKET

PLUG

PLATYPUS WHEEL

USELESS BUTTONS
(ALL OVER)

ROGUE CRICKET BAT
LEFT ON FLOOR

Celina laughed maniacally with glee. The platypuses joined in and growled maniacally too. It was a complete din.

Then, as if on cue, Arctic Thunder and Millie Monday showed up. Millie was looking incredibly happy (it was a Monday, after all).

The Platypus Kid could see them on a security monitor – they were outside the warehouse. She had left the door unlocked to speed things up a little, but it took them a full ten minutes to figure out how to open it anyway. They banged and clattered at the door in their attempt – even if she hadn't been expecting them, she would have had ample time to prepare.

'Surprise!' shouted Arctic Thunder triumphantly, having finally made it through the door.

'We figured out exactly where you were hiding, Platypus Kid, and we made it past your advanced security system!' added Millie Monday.

'Congratulations!' replied the Platypus Kid, clapping sarcastically. 'You truly are incredible. However, now you are my prisoners and—'

But before she could finish, another superhero appeared, and then another, and another.

'You spend ages waiting for a superhero to fall into your trap ... and then they all come along at once,' Celina said.

'What do you mean by trap?' asked Arctic Thunder, looking suspiciously around the warehouse.

The Platypus Kid decided to delay her grand reveal until all the superheroes had arrived. One by one they flew, swooped and triumphantly strolled into the cave – into her trap.

'Right, is that everyone?' she asked, counting each superhero on her fingers before deciding to give up when she reached ten.

'Grrr,' said a platypus, nodding knowingly.

'OK, excellent. As I was saying, you are now all my prisoners … and BEFORE you start laughing ...' she added quickly, launching a raw chicken at Millie Monday.

Millie went to use her laser vision to turn the chicken into charcoal, but nothing happened.

Well, that's not strictly true, something happened. A raw chicken hit her square in the face.

'As demonstrated, by me, the Platypus Kid, none of your powers work in here, not even mine. Well, to be entirely accurate, none of your powers will work in *there* thanks to the forcefield from my Superpower Neutraliser Machine.' As the Platypus Kid said this, a series of steel bars fell from the ceiling and rose from the ground to create one large prison cell, trapping every hero inside.

'Have we got our transformorphic calculations correct?' asked one of her platypuses.

'I have no idea what that means,' replied the Platypus Kid.

'But you can understand me?'

'No, I don't understand you.'

‘I mean, you can understand what I’m saying?’

‘NO, I CAN’T! I don’t know what trans-fam-ofia calculations are!’ The Platypus Kid was beginning to turn red.

‘Sorry, it means that the Superpower Neutraliser Machine is no longer working out here, but is working inside the prison cell. Like you asked for.’

‘Oh. Well, is it?’

‘Well, we are having a conversation, so it’s not working out here.’

‘And they’re still locked in the cell so it’s not working in there! I did it! I am amazing!’ screamed the Platypus Kid, jumping for joy.

In that moment, the platypuses learnt

something very important. It wasn't because they couldn't communicate with platypuses that humans stole their inventions. It was because they were horribly selfish.

'If I had my powers right now, I would melt these bars, fly you up into the sky and drop you in the river. You won't get away with this!' screamed Millie Monday, looking incredibly upset (which was very rare on a Monday).

'I already have,' the Platypus Kid said, launching her head back before letting out an evil laugh. 'There is no one left to stop me. No one at all.'

HOW ABOUT A TRIPLE CHEESE PIZZA?

Dylan woke up the next morning to find the iguanas asleep. All of them, that is, except Crazy Red-Eye Paul, who was sitting on top of the toilet-roll house chewing his foreleg. (He liked to alternate between his arm and his leg. Different textures, different flavours.)

'I see you're awake' said Red-Eye. He

stopped chewing his foreleg and jumped off the toilet-roll house, quietly stepping over the sleeping iguanas to reach the other side of the cage.

'Look, kid, I'm sorry we weren't truthful with you from the—'

Red-Eye didn't get the chance to finish his thought. Once again, the TV burst into life to show a smiling Platypus Kid.

'I TOLD YOU WHAT I WOULD DO, BUT YOU JUST LAUGHED AT ME. PEOPLE ALWAYS LAUGH AT ME, BUT NOT ANY MORE. BEHOLD, ALL THE WORLD'S SUPERHEROES ARE POWERLESS TO STOP ME. THEY ARE LOCKED BEHIND BARS!'

The camera zoomed out to show a prison cell, full of superheroes. Dylan moved closer to the TV, staring in disbelief.

Standing guard, holding what looked like cricket bats (they were cricket bats), was an army of what looked like angry-looking platypuses (they were angry ... you get the point).

It was hard to see anyone Dylan recognised at first – there were hundreds of superheroes, in fact all the superheroes in the world had turned up. Dylan looked closely at the TV and eventually spotted his brother and sister.

At a second glance he noticed Atomic Adam, a superhero who could produce explosions with the fluff from his belly button, and he noticed that the Platypus Kid had even caught Terrifying Suzanne.

Yes, all of the world's superheroes were behind bars. One by one, they had travelled to the Platypus Kid's lair to try to save the world, and one by one they had underestimated her skills and been captured. One by one … until there were none left.

'NOW I HAVE EVERY SUPERHERO TRAPPED BEHIND BARS, PERHAPS YOU WILL START BELIEVING THAT TOMORROW, MY BEAUTIFUL PLATYPUSES AND I WILL TAKE OVER THE WORLD. AND THEN NO ONE WILL TELL ME WHAT TO DO. NOT EVER AGAIN. HA! HA! HA!'

The television faded to black once more, before cutting back to the same newsreader in the studio. He once again looked confused – perhaps even worried this time, too.

'But she can still only talk to platypuses! HA! HA! HA!' At that moment, a platypus holding a cricket bat waddled into the studio and hit the newsreader on the shoulder with its webbed foot. The platypus then went over to the camera and, with an almighty webbed-foot-slap, smashed the studio camera. The picture on the TV abruptly cut out.

'TOMORROW? Guys! Wake up,' said Dylan, falling over his bed to get to the iguanas' cage. 'Guys, WAKE UP NOW!'

The rest of the iguanas woke with a start. 'What is it?' asked Paul, still lying down with his eyes closed.

'Have you got us more lemonade?' added Smelly Paul.

'No more lemonade. Not until we save the WORLD!'

As one, the iguanas started laughing hysterically. It seemed to be a bit of a theme that arose whenever Dylan talked about being a superhero, or when he talked about saving the world. Or when he talked about wanting a cape. In fact, they pretty much laughed at everything he suggested.

'The Platypus Kid plans to take over the world tomorrow. Every superhero in the world has been captured. Every superhero except one.'

'Iguana Boy?' asked Paul.

'IGUANA BOY,' said Dylan, as triumphantly as possible.

The iguanas started laughing again, but this time Dylan ignored them. He jumped onto his bed with his hands on his hips ... but hit his head on the light above him and plonked down inelegantly on the mattress (you can guess how the iguanas reacted to that).

'Kid, you ain't no superhero. You can talk to iguanas – that's it! Face facts, buddy, you are a laughing stock,' said Paul (whilst laughing, as if to prove his point).

'But the Platypus Kid can only talk to platypuses, and no one's laughing now.'

'Apart from that newsreader – he was still laughing,' said Pauline.

'Yeah, and to be honest, we still find it quite funny,' added Smelly Paul.

'OK, they are still laughing, but look at what she's achieved.' Dylan moved closer to the iguanas, getting onto his knees so he could look them directly in the eye (although he didn't want to get too close, as Smelly Paul really did smell). 'Now is the time for me to fulfil my destiny. To become the superhero I have always dreamed of being. It's time for me to use my power for the benefit of all mankind.'

'I just don't see how, kid. You were right – we're doomed' said Paul, turning away from Dylan.

'Don't put Dylan down, we're not doomed. We just need a plan,' said Pauline.

'Any ideas?' Paul said. 'Because I'm struggling to see how a boy and four iguanas can break into a secret warehouse and rescue a bunch of powerless superheroes that are guarded by an army of platypuses armed with cricket bats.'

The next few hours went by painfully slowly. They needed a plan and they needed it, well, to be perfectly honest, a few hours ago. It was getting close to lunch and they had nothing to show for it. Tomorrow the Platypus Kid would make her attempt to take over the world, and Dylan was the only superhero left to stop her.

Dylan sighed dramatically. It was bugging him that he didn't know exactly how long he had to save the world. The Platypus Kid had said 'tomorrow'. He wished she had been a little more specific. *When* tomorrow? He reckoned that taking over the world was more of an evening thing, so, probably after dinner – surely she wouldn't want to take over the world on an empty stomach ...?

These were guesses, of course: he knew nothing about taking over the world, nor did his sweet-looking, and, as he had recently discovered, sweet-natured iguanas. And to make matters worse, reports of crimes were increasing all over the city, with no superheroes around to stop them or save the day.

Every crime Dylan could think of, from a stolen handbag, to breaking zoo animals out, to dropping litter on the pavement (yes, that *is* a crime), had gone up rapidly since the superheroes had been taken hostage, and there wasn't a single superhero left in the world who could do a darn thing about it.

Talking of not being able to do a darn thing about it, Dylan and his iguanas were still desperately trying to come up with a plan.

Despite his reservations, it was Paul who had had the first idea.

'I have an idea,' said Paul. 'And I think it's the best plan I have ever had ...'

'Go for it,' said Dylan, hopefully.

'We break them out.'

Crazy Red-Eye Paul started clapping. He was impressed.

'Great plan, Paul.' Dylan nodded. 'Good to see you getting on board. The only slight problem I can see is that isn't technically a plan.'

'What do you mean?'

'A plan is how you are going to achieve what you set out to do. A plan needs steps. Step one, do this, step two, do that. Breaking them out is the end result. Therefore "break them out" isn't a plan, unfortunately.' He smiled at the iguana.

'Oh. Well. I can't be expected to think of every single detail. You can fill in the blanks,' said Paul.

'I have a plan,' said Smelly Paul. 'Step one, we find some huge dinosaurs. Step two, we tame them, teach them the way of the iguana. Step three, once they are ready, we ride on their backs into the warehouse, they eat the platypuses and break the superheroes out of the cage.'

Red-Eye actually stood up on his back legs to clap this idea.

Dylan stifled a groan. 'Again, an A+ for effort, Smelly Paul, but I see a couple of problems.'

'Be honest with me, Dylan, I can take criticism.'

'OK, well, firstly – dinosaurs are extinct.

Have been for millions of years.'

'I see. I did not know that. Please continue.'

'Secondly, if we did, by some miracle, find a dinosaur, I doubt we could tame them. Even if we could, it would take months, if not years. We have until tomorrow night to save the world.'

'Well, next time I won't even bother,' said Smelly Paul, turning and storming off in a huff. (Dylan made a mental note that Smelly Paul was not good at taking criticism and moved on swiftly.)

'I have a plan,' said Pauline.

'Go on then,' said Dylan, trying to sound hopeful again (he wasn't).

'Everyone likes pizza. Everyone also

eats pizza. My plan is we deliver a pizza to the lair …'

'Woah, hold on a minute,' interrupted Red-Eye. 'What kind of pizza?'

'Does that really matter?' said Dylan. 'I don't see how—'

'Does that matter? DOES THAT MATTER?!' screamed Red-Eye, his big red eye growing even larger.

'It's a simple cheese pizza, Paul,' said Pauline, keen to calm him down and get on with the rest of her plan.

'SIMPLE CHEESE PIZZA?' screamed Red-Eye. 'There is no such thing. What kind of cheese, how many cheeses? I won't eat anything with fewer than three different cheeses—'

'Fine, it's a triple-cheese pizza!' snapped Pauline, who was getting frustrated.

'Three cheeses? Nice …' said Red-Eye, who spent the next thirty seconds daydreaming about pizza, rather than listening to the plan.

'The Platypus Kid will be so excited she'll take the pizza inside her secret warehouse … and we will be waiting inside the box,' said Pauline.

'Won't she find a pizza that she didn't order randomly turning up at her secret hideout suspicious?' asked Dylan, dubiously.

'No one suspects a triple-cheese pizza. They just eat it.'

'OK, once you're inside, what do you do?'

Pauline paused. She clearly hadn't thought this far ahead. 'We get out of the box and then ... we do Paul's plan!'

'The pizza gets us in, then we break the superheroes out. Genius!' said Paul.

Dylan looked around the room. Crazy Red-Eye Paul was dancing like crazy (he really liked the plan), Pauline and Paul were high-fiving, while Smelly Paul was mumbling to himself in the corner – he didn't think his plan had been given enough attention. They were getting nowhere fast, and Dylan knew he had to make a very difficult and spontaneous decision.

'We can't carry on like this, none of these plans work,' he said, rubbing his forehead with the sweaty palm of his hand (he thought if he rubbed hard enough, maybe it would block out the constant stream of terrible ideas). 'We are no closer to having a plan, and even if we came up with the perfect plan—'

'I like the pizza one' said Red-Eye, interrupting rather unhelpfully. Dylan ignored him.

'Even if we did have the perfect plan, we don't know where the Platypus Kid is or what she is planning on doing!' he said.

The iguanas paused. They hadn't really considered this. For once they had nothing to say.

'I need to concentrate on figuring out

where she is so that we can stop her. That's why I am handing over the responsibility of the plan to you.' Dylan looked sternly at the iguanas.

The iguanas all looked behind themselves to see who Dylan was talking to. Luckily, there was a mirror behind them, which sped up their realisation somewhat. They gasped.

Dylan almost gave up hope there and then.

'Us?' said Paul, just to confirm.

'Yes. All of you. As you know, I have wanted to be a superhero my entire life. What I've realised is that I can't do it alone. I need you guys to help me save the world. I know that right now things aren't looking great. It's hard to see how four iguanas and a kid can save the world. But I know that we can, if we just work together.'

'We've got a lot of work to do ...' said Paul, and with that the four iguanas huddled into a circle and began to create the most ingenious plan the world had ever known.

Or, more accurately, what they thought was the most ingenious plan the world had ever known ...

OK, to be 100-per-cent, arrow-in-the-bull's-eye, you-sunk-my-battleship accurate, what they hoped was the most ingenious plan the world had ever known.

Probably. (Possibly.)

Penguin
PIZZA
HOT!!
PLEASE DO NOT BEND

Have you ever been mind-numbingly bored? So bored that you almost wanted to cry in frustration? The kind of boredom that can only come from something incredibly exciting just over the horizon ...

The Platypus Kid was mind-numbingly bored. Sitting around all day in a huge, boring warehouse waiting for something to happen was pretty boring. Even more so when you were waiting to take over the world. Why did she have to say she would do it tomorrow? Tomorrow felt like a lifetime away ...

She shouldn't have put a time on it – she could have just said, 'And soon I will take over the world ...' and kept everyone guessing a little. After all, her plan was already in place, her army of platypuses strategically positioned all over the world outside palaces, castles and stately homes, ready to capture the world's leaders.

'It's tomorrow in Australia,' she said, looking hopefully at her platypuses (although if you were to ask an Australian, they would probably tell you it was today). They didn't look impressed. Here's another thing you need to know about the humble platypus – they are a supremely honourable animal. The Platypus Kid had said tomorrow. In London, it was still today, and a platypus always keeps their word (or their growl, if you can't understand them. A platypus always keeps their growl).

The Platypus Kid, despite her name, was of course not a platypus, but nonetheless she intended to wait until tomorrow. She thought about setting her alarm early, but decided against it. Taking over the world was more of an evening thing. After dinner, she thought.

To pass the time, she played all manner of board games with her platypuses. Despite making one poor strategic move after another, she won every time. The platypuses had learnt the hard way that she wasn't the best loser: in Connect 4, they would only ever connect three; in Monopoly, they only bought the stations; in Pie Face they would keep turning the dial until, well, they had pie on their face; they would KerPlunk in KerPlunk and Jenga in Jenga, but the Platypus Kid didn't suspect a thing.

'They're letting you win, you know,' said Arctic Thunder from behind the metal bars of the huge cage in which they were trapped.

The superheroes were slumped against the back wall of the prison cell, apart from Arctic Thunder and Millie Monday, who were standing up, their heads resting on the bars.

'What did you say?' asked the Platypus Kid.

'Your platypuses – they've been letting you win for the past two hours.'

'No, we haven't, I promise!' replied one of

the platypuses desperately.

'I know, don't worry. I know when a superhero is trying to strike up a conversation in order to escape. It's a classic superhero trick. You think I haven't read all the stories about you, Arctic Thunder?'

'I'm not sure what you mean ...'

'You know exactly what I mean. If you spent more time saving people and less time boasting about your fairly minimal achievements, then perhaps you wouldn't be in this mess. You give all your strategies away when you boast about how amazing you are! I know all about Arctic Thunder versus Elastiloco ...'

I HAVE YOU NOW, ARCTIC THUNDER!
YES, YOU DO. IT'S A SHAME, THOUGH ...
WHAT'S A SHAME?
IT'S JUST ... NEVER MIND.
AT
TELL ME!
WELL, IT'S JUST, LOOKING DOWN ON YOUR BEAUTIFUL TRAP FROM UP HERE, IT'S REALLY INCREDIBLE, I MUST SAY.
AT
YOU THINK SO?
OH, ABSOLUTELY! THE CAGE, THE BOILING WATER ... AND THE SPIKES AROUND THE EDGE ...? NICE TOUCH.
AT
THANK YOU. THEY WERE A LAST-MINUTE ADDITION.
THEY REALLY BRING THE DANGER TO LIFE. IT'S JUST A SHAME THAT YOU'RE ALL THE WAY DOWN THERE AND CAN'T SHARE THIS BEAUTIFUL VIEW.
AT
OH, BUT I DON'T HAVE TO BE ...

YOU'RE RIGHT, IT REALLY DOES LOOK FANTASTIC FROM UP HERE! MY MOTHER WOULD BE SO PROUD ...

‘I was just trying to stop you from being embarrassed,’ Arctic continued. ‘Your platypuses are making a fool out of you.’

‘Yeah, he was just trying to help you,’ said Millie Monday (who, by the way, was very unhappy at having her powers taken away on a Monday. She was used to that every other day of the week, but not on Mondays). ‘Those things are really ugly by the way,’ she added, pointing at the platypuses. ‘Almost as ugly as you.’

‘Oh, here we go, right on time.’ The Platypus Kid turned to Millie. ‘Is it your turn now? Trying to get me angry? I know your history, too – Millie Monday versus Bangers and Mash.’

MILLIE MONDAY HAD BEEN CAUGHT BY THE EVIL SUPERVILLAIN TWINS, BANGERS AND MASH.
SOON WE WILL CAUSE MAYHEM ALL OVER THE WORLD, MASH.
THAT'S RIGHT, BANGERS! NO ONE CAN STOP US NOW, NOT EVEN MILLIE MONDAY!
YOUR PLAN IS STUPID
WHAT DID YOU SAY?
YOUR PLAN. IT'S STUPID. A BRAINLESS SLUG COULD COME UP WITH A BETTER PLAN.
WE HAVEN'T EVEN TOLD YOU OUR PLAN.
BET IT'S STUPID, THOUGH.
USING MY POWERS TO CAUSE HUGE BANGS, I WILL BLOW UP THE ENTIRE INTERNET, THEN NO ONE WILL BE ABLE TO GO ON GOOGLE EVER AGAIN!
THAT'S RIGHT, AND I WILL COVER EVERY SINGLE MOUNTAIN WITH MASHED POTATO!
WAIT, YOUR POWER IS TO CREATE MASHED POTATO?

YES, IT IS. WITNESS MY AWESOME POWER!
AND WITH EVERY MOUNTAIN COVERED IN POTATO, NO ONE WILL EVER BE ABLE TO SKI AGAIN!
HE CAME UP WITH THAT PLAN ON HIS OWN, BY THE WAY. I HAD NO PART IN IT ...
I THOUGHT BY YOUR NAME YOU WERE ABLE TO DO SOMETHING IMPRESSIVE, LIKE MASHING METAL. NOT MAKING HORRIBLE MASHED POTATO ...
HEY, IT'S NOT HORRIBLE, IT'S LOVELY.
IT'S DISGUSTING.
YOU HAVEN'T TRIED MINE – HERE, HAVE A BITE.
WELL, YOU'LL NEED TO UNTIE ME FIRST.
SURE, HERE YOU GO.

YOU FOOLS! THE INTERNET WILL LIVE TO FIGHT ANOTHER DAY AND NO ONE WILL HAVE TO CANCEL THEIR SKI TRIP THIS WINTER, THANKS TO MILLIE MONDAY!

'I know all your tricks. That goes for all of you!' said the Platypus Kid, addressing all the superheroes. 'I have studied every little trick you have ever done, even the unsuccessful ones. Honestly, Millie, keeping up with the day of the week shouldn't be that hard – just look at my socks,' said the Platypus Kid, lifting up her trousers to show off a snazzy pair of yellow socks with the word 'Friday' written on them.

The Platypus Kid casually walked over to the table, and placed a yellow counter down on the Monopoly board. 'Connect Four,' she said, walking away triumphantly to the cheers (or growls, for everyone else) of her platypuses. She had become the first person in the history of the world to win Monopoly with a Connect 4 piece (she only connected three).

But the Platypus Kid had done her homework on every superhero. She was confident that not a single one of them would be able to stop her.

★ ★ SPOILER ALERT ★ ★

She was absolutely right. Not a single one of them would ...

IGUANA BOY TO THE RESCUE

Dylan just didn't know where to start. He had heard every great story throughout history when it came to superheroes, but the one thing they always seemed to leave out was how they tracked down the villain in the first place. It turned out that supervillains didn't leave a map or place a big neon arrow over their location. You'd be forgiven for thinking they didn't want to be found.

Dylan's first thought was to check the broadcast footage. He had rightly assumed that this was filmed in the Platypus Kid's lair. He listened in vain for a secret code. He zoomed in on the reflection in her eyes to see if he could see where she was – all he saw was a camera. He even looked at the table behind to see if there was a letter with her address on, but so far he had found nothing.

He could tell her lair was by a river, but having studied geography at school he knew there were at least ten rivers across the world. (There are, in fact, many more rivers than just ten, but Dylan hadn't learnt about those yet.)

Dylan kept drawing a blank. Finally, he decided he had no choice but to break a promise he had made to his brother whilst in a supremely tight headlock: that he would never enter Sam's room.

Arctic Thunder – or Sam, as Dylan much preferred to call him so as to not inflate his ego even further – was a very private person. There were fifteen different signs on the door, all variations of the same message: 'Keep Out'. (Seven of them named Dylan in person.)

This was an emergency, however. His brother (or, more importantly, the world) was in trouble and there could be a vital clue inside, which could lead him directly to the Platypus Kid.

To Dylan's surprise, the door opened with ease. He had expected a lock to pick, or, as he didn't know how to pick a lock, that he might need to break the door down himself. But it was open. The room was that of a typical teenager. There was a photo of Atomic Adam's Atomobile, and a picture of a superhero called Lacey Shoestring.

As well as making fireworks out of the fluff in his belly button, in his spare time, Atomic Adam liked to stop petty crimes.

PETTY CRIME 1: FOULING
BANG!
PETTY CRIME 2: LITTERING
BOOM!
PETTY CRIME 3:
ILLEGAL PARKING
POW!

And Lacey Shoestring? Well, she had the ability to tie shoelaces just by looking at them. (She was working hard to figure out a way of untying them too, but it was proving difficult.)

SUPERHERO COLLECTIVE HQ ID PASS

NAME: LACEY

AKA: LACEY SHOESTRING

SUPERPOWER: TYING SHOE-LACES WITH HER MIND

AGE/HEIGHT: 15/5ft 5ins

DISGUISE: KNEE-HIGH BOOTS

FAVOURITE FOOTWEAR: FLIP-FLOPS

I WAS RUNNING AFTER THIS HUGE CRIMINAL ... I MEAN SUPERVILLAIN ... IN FACT, THERE WERE FOUR ... TY ... FORTY OF THEM, AND I TRIPPED

Dylan stood at one end of his brother's bedroom. Arctic's bed hovered in the middle of the room, held up by tiny hurricanes that he had created himself. Dylan would have loved a bed like that but unfortunately they don't sell them in Ikea (hurricanes are notoriously difficult to flat-pack).

Dylan had never been in Sam's room unaccompanied before and always felt on edge during the rare occasions he was invited in, so he had never really looked around.

The walls were sky blue with clouds painted towards the top and on the ceiling. The lamps and light shade hanging from the ceiling were all in the shape of lightning bolts, while above his desk was a small rain cloud that trickled down over a beautiful bonsai tree. The heat from the lamp on his desk dried off the water, creating a microclimate water feature.

Dylan moved over to the desk, careful not to disturb anything – even if he could somehow save his brother and the world, if Sam discovered he had been in his room, it would be the end of Dylan's world ...

On the desk was his laptop computer. Dylan opened it and was met by a password screen. *Fiddlesticks*, thought Dylan. He tried 'fiddlesticks' but it didn't work. He wasn't exactly sure why he tried the first word that came into his head and, in all honesty, he had wasted one of his attempts. The prompt on the screen said he had four attempts left.

Next he tried 'Arctic Thunder', thinking his brother was vain enough to use his own name. Three attempts left. 'Elastiloco' – his biggest triumph had been capturing his first supervillain. Two attempts left. He had to be careful now. He looked around the room for inspiration.

Maybe it was 'Lacey Shoestring' – he certainly seemed to like her. Or 'Atomobile' – his favourite car. He tried that.

He was down to his final attempt.

'What could it be ...?' said Dylan, thinking out loud. His brother didn't really share much with him, so it was hard to guess what he would use for his password. Then something popped into his head. It was a long shot. A last, desperate attempt. 'Surely not ...' said Dylan, as he entered nine letters into the keyboard.

S P A R T A C U S

Password accepted.

'I guess he cared for you more than he let on, Paul, even if he did throw you at me,' Dylan said, out loud. Making a mental note to tell the iguana of his discovery, he then opened Sam's laptop and refreshed his latest internet browser. It brought up a map of Central London. He could see where Superhero HQ was, and, a little further along, right on the bank of the River Thames, was a large warehouse with a little pin on it.

This had to be where they were.

All of a sudden a small box in the bottom right-hand corner of the screen popped up, startling Dylan. A man in his early forties with a silver goatee beard and slicked-back hair, was frantically tapping on the screen.

'Arctic ... Arctic? Is that you ...?'

'Hello?' said Dylan.

'It is! Oh, thank heavens. I thought we

were doomed. I knew he wouldn't capture my bravest, most heroic—'

'Let me stop you there,' said Dylan, who was beginning to feel nauseous at hearing such high praise for his brother. 'I'm not Arctic Thunder. I'm his brother.'

The man on the screen sighed heavily and hung his head.

'Then I suppose ...'

'Yes. He has been captured by the Platypus Kid.'

'So I was right. We are doomed.'

'Who are you, mister?' asked Dylan, making the window bigger on the screen. In doing so he realised who it was, and that the man needed no introduction (but he proceeded to give one anyway).

'The name is Ron Strongman. I am the head of the Superhero Collective. At least I was, until the Platypus Kid captured every superhero in the world.'

'Not every superhero,' said Dylan, rolling up his sleeves.

'You don't mean ...?'

'Yes, I do. I recently discovered my powers, I have figured out where the Platypus Kid is hiding, and I have a top team working on a super awesome plan as we speak.'

Ron Strongman slowly looked up. A small smile began to form on his lips as his hopes rose. 'What's your name, kid? What can you do?'

Dylan put his hands on his hips, looked to the side and said: 'I'm Iguana Boy, Mr Strongman. I can talk to iguanas.'

The screen went dead.

If Dylan was being cynical, he might

think that upon hearing of his power, Ron Strongman had cut the connection himself (if he was super-cynical, it may have been tears of laughter dripping onto the keyboard that broke the computer). But Dylan didn't have time to be cynical. He had to save the world.

And you know what? He was feeling pretty good. He had discovered a supervillain's whereabouts all by himself. Now all he needed to do was figure out how to travel across London with his iguanas, break into a top-secret hideout and free all the world's superheroes.

(And he still didn't have a cape.)

Dylan opened the desk drawer to find a pen and paper so he could jot down the address.

Inside he found what he was looking for, along with a map for the underground train in London.

Dylan ran back to his room where he found the iguanas clapping ferociously. Paul was in front of them, bowing.

'It's genius, Paul. It truly is genius,' said Pauline.

'I take it you have a plan, then?' said Dylan.

'Only the greatest plan the world has ever seen,' replied Red-Eye, giving Paul a high five.

'Great, you can explain it to me on the way. We need to leave, NOW!'

And so Dylan, the Pauls and Pauline, left

10 Wilshere Close in search of the Platypus Kid's secret warehouse hideout on the banks of the River Thames.

Dylan had ridden the underground tube train many times with his parents, but this was the first time he had done so on his own. Luckily, the station was only a few minutes' walk from his house. Using the map, he and his friends had managed to make it across London to Embankment, which was the name of the closest tube station to the Platypus Kid's warehouse – it was only half a mile from the stop. They were almost there.

'Wait,' said Dylan, suddenly. 'I've just

remembered, you haven't even told me what the plan is yet.'

'Oh, it's a crazy plan' said Paul, touching Dylan's hand. 'So crazy, it just might work ...'

IGUANA BOY SAVES THE WORLD

'Well, that didn't work,' said Dylan some time later, removing his penguin mask and rubbing his head where he had been hit by a cricket-bat-waving platypus.

(In Paul's defence, he had said his plan was crazy and that it *just might work*. He had offered no guarantees.)

The floor beneath Dylan was cold and hard, but when he tried sitting up his head pounded even harder, as if someone was playing a set of steel drums inside his skull.

'I think he's waking up,' said Atomic Adam.

'DOES ANYONE KNOW WHO HE IS?!' shouted Terrifying Suzanne.

'Not a clue,' said Millie Monday and Arctic Thunder, practically at the same time. Their non-superhero kid brother turning up and failing to rescue them. How embarrassing ...

'Let me help you,' said Atomic Adam, offering his hand to help Dylan off the floor. Dylan's vision was beginning to return, but his memory was still hazy.

He was in a cell. That rang a bell (which

really didn't help his headache). He had been going somewhere to do something important and it had had something to do with rescuing people ...

He was there to get people out. That was it. So why was he inside ...? It all came flooding back to him like an overflowing bubble bath. He was there to SAVE THE WORLD. Suddenly Dylan realised he would soon be greeted by a real-life SUPPERVILLAIN! He decided that being in disguise might actually come in handy, so he reluctantly put his penguin mask back on.

The plan hadn't gone ... well, according to plan. And now he was stuck in the very cell from which he had been meant to be rescuing people.

And to make matters worse, he was dressed like a penguin …

'What's your name, kid?' asked Atomic Adam.

'It's Dylan,' said Arctic Thunder with a sigh, walking over to his brother and picking

him up by his, well, his penguin outfit. 'We might as well admit it. He's our annoying kid brother. What are you doing here, Dylan?'

'I came here to save the ... world.' As the words escaped his mouth, Dylan realised, much like Paul with his own leg, he might have bitten off more than he could chew.

'Ah, a fellow superhero. Fell for the same trap we did. No shame there,' said Atomic Adam, patting him on the back.

'He is not a superhero,' said Millie, sourly. 'And he never will be.'

'Unless I was right when I was teasing you at home,' said Arctic Thunder.

Dylan slumped to the floor.

'Right about what?' asked Millie.

'He has a power!' said Arctic, sneeringly. 'Only, whatever it is, he's too ashamed to admit to it! So, he thought he would come here and try to save us, to prove he is a real hero. Instead, he's been captured ... like the failure he is,' finished his brother.

'You were captured, too!' screamed Dylan, slightly taking his brother by surprise. 'And, yes, you're right – are you happy? I do have a power and I didn't want to tell you about it and I thought maybe, just maybe, I could come here and prove to you that I am a real hero. But instead, I'm in here. With you.'

'Don't beat yourself up!' said Atomic Adam kindly, to the clear displeasure of Arctic Thunder and Millie Monday. 'You tried and, look at it this way, you got as far as any of us, including your brother and sister.' He smiled at Dylan. 'So, what do you call yourself, kid? My name is Atomic Adam. It's nice to meet you.'

'My name is … well … I'm Iguana Boy.'

Arctic Thunder and Millie Monday both looked at each other, very confused.

'Iguana Boy, you say? Can you turn into an iguana? Maybe sneak through the bars and hit that big button on the Superpower Neutraliser Machine to get us out?' suggested Atomic Adam.

'Our powers don't work in here, have you forgotten that, YOU FOOL?!' screamed Terrifying Suzanne.

'My mistake ... haven't had to use them in a while,' said Adam.

'I would have blown the door down with a tornado by now if we could use our powers. That machine is stopping pur powers from working,' said Arctic Thunder.

'Yeah, or I would have melted the bars with my eyes by now. You know, if we'd waited until it was Monday,' added Millie Monday.

'OK, so what can you do, kid? Change colour?' asked Atomic Adam.

'That's chameleons! Don't you know anything? YOU FOOL!' screamed Terrifying Suzanne. (She really was terrifying.)

'Suzanne still seems to have her power

intact,' said Atomic Adam, moving away from her at speed.

'I can't do any of those things ... I-I can talk to them,' said Dylan, looking down at his penguin feet.

'Talk to who?' asked Adam.

'... Iguanas.'

The laughter was loud. It was the loudest laughter Dylan had ever heard. The noise made him feel sick and his head throbbed uncontrollably. Everyone laughed, except Atomic Adam, who clearly felt sorry for him.

'You're such an embarrassment, Dylan. I would roast you like a chicken if we weren't locked in this force field,' said

Millie Monday.

'And if it was a Monday,' added Arctic Thunder, snidely. 'What did I say to you, Dylan? You will never be a superhero! You should have listened to me.'

'Wait, it's not Monday? How long have I been knocked out? said Dylan, suddenly panicking.

'A few hours, I would guess. It's Tuesday morning.'

'It's tomorrow?'

'No, it's today, YOU FOOL!' said Terrifying Suzanne, correcting Dylan. She was right, of course, but Dylan was talking about the metaphorical tomorrow of yesterday ... To be clear, he was talking about the day the

Platypus Kid would take over the world.

'Leave him alone!' shouted a voice from outside the cage.

Dylan looked up to see the Platypus Kid. She was smaller than Dylan had expected. She was wearing that VERY distracting yellow mask again. There was something familiar about her voice now he had met her in person but he couldn't quite put his finger on it.

She continued: 'He puts the rest of you to shame. He doesn't have some super fancy power like being able to fly, or to create fireworks from his belly button. Despite having very little to use against me, he was fearless and gave it his best shot.' The

Platypus Kid approached the cage cautiously, to avoid being grabbed by Arctic Thunder, like Elastiloco had been. 'Although I'm not sure about the whole penguin thing ...'

'THAT WAS GOING TO BE MY NEXT QUESTION, ACTUALLY. WHY ARE YOU DRESSED AS A PENGUIN?' said Terrifying Suzanne. (Well, she shouted the question, really, through teeth gritted in a continuous snarl.)

'I assumed that's what an iguana looks like,' said Atomic Adam.

'I assumed it was all part of your "master plan",' said Arctic Thunder, with a bucket-load of sarcasm.

'Oh, I love a good plan,' said Atomic

Adam, sitting down cross-legged in front of Dylan. 'Let's hear it then – I hope it works out!'

'Well, let me tell it to you all word for word,' Dylan began ...

THE PLAN: THE IGUANAS AND DYLAN, OUTSIDE THE WAREHOUSE

DYLAN: 'SO, WHAT'S THE PLAN?'

PAUL: 'I THINK IT'S EASIER IF WE SHOW YOU. JUST DO EVERYTHING WE SAY AND DON'T ASK ANY QUESTIONS, OK?'

DYLAN: 'FINE, BUT WE NEED TO HURRY. WHAT DO WE DO FIRST?'

RED-EYE: 'YOU DRESS UP AS A PENGUIN. HERE'S YOUR OUTFIT.'

DYLAN: 'I DON'T UNDERSTAND ...'

PAUL: 'NO QUESTIONS, JUST TRUST US! PUT IT ON.'

SMELLY PAUL: 'OK, NOW WE NEED THE BOXES OF COOKIES.'

DYLAN: 'WHY DO WE NEED BOXES OF COOKIES AND WHY—?'

PAUL: 'JUST TAKE THE COOKIES.'

DYLAN IS STANDING DRESSED AS A PENGUIN, HOLDING COOKIES, WITH THE IGUANAS OUTSIDE THE FRONT DOOR OF THE WAREHOUSE.

RED-EYE: 'OK. NOW HERE'S THE REAL GENIUS OF THIS PLAN - WE PRESS THE DOORBELL.'

DYLAN: 'ARE YOU MAD? WHY WOULD WE PRESS THE DOORBELL—?'

PAUL: 'JUST PRESS THE DOORBELL.'

PAUL PUSHES DYLAN'S FINGER INTO THE

DOORBELL. THEY STAND MOTIONLESS, WAITING.

RED-EYE: 'YOU KNOW WHAT, ON SECOND THOUGHTS, THIS IS A TERRIBLE PLAN.'

DYLAN: 'WHAT?'

PAUL: 'YEAH, THIS ISN'T GOING TO WORK AT ALL.'

SMELLY PAUL: **'BAIL?'**

ALL THE IGUANAS DROP THEIR COOKIES AND RUN AWAY, LEAVING DYLAN AT THE DOOR. IT OPENS AND A PLATYPUS HOLDING A CRICKET BAT APPEARS.

DYLAN: 'UMM ... WOULD YOU LIKE TO BUY SOME COOKIES FROM A PENGUIN?'

THUD. DYLAN IS HIT BY A CRICKET BAT.

'Did it work?' asked Atomic Adam, with genuine sincerity.

'Yes,' said Dylan, with not so much as a bucket of sarcasm, but a truckload.

'Brilliant! We're free! Take that, Platypus Kid!'

A single look from Terrifying Suzanne was all it took for Atomic Adam to realise that the plan had, in fact, not worked at all. He quietly shuffled back against the bars, raising his hand apologetically.

'Ah, the old penguin cookie seller trick,' said Millie Monday, with a knowing smile. 'I haven't seen that used since ... actually, I have never seen that used. Come to think of it, I have no idea what it is at all.'

Dylan knew that the reason Millie Monday had never seen it used before was because it was a terrible plan. It made no sense. Why penguins? Why cookies? And what had they expected to happen when the door opened? And then they had run away, leaving him on his own.

The worst thing about it, though, Dylan realised, was that it made it look like it was his idea.

The Platypus Kid had been listening intently to Dylan's story. She could sense the desperation to fit in with his fellow superheroes, a desperation that had driven him to what was quite possibly the worst plan the world had ever seen. But there was something else … another reason she had been listening so intently … It almost felt as if she recognised his voice. She never forgot the voice of someone who told her what to do, even if it was muffled behind a terrible penguin mask …

'Wait, Dylan … is that you?' she asked.

Dylan was shocked. He knew one of the most important rules of superheroes was: 'Never reveal your secret identity', but he never expected anyone to guess just like that. (Especially not the very first supervillain he came across. Another embarrassment.)

'I … uh … no … Dylan?' He wasn't very convincing.

'Yes, Dylan Spencer. It is you. I never forget the voice of ANYONE who tells me what to do!'

Dylan had a flashback to that one day at school when he had sat next to a strange girl.

'Celina? You're the Platypus Kid?'

'Yes, it is I, Celina Shufflebottom.'

The superheroes all sniggered at her name. (In their defence, it is a pretty funny name.)

'Stop laughing!' Celina yelled suddenly. 'I outsmarted all of you! How dare you laugh at me!'

'Why are you doing this? I don't understand. You seemed like such a nice girl at school,' replied Dylan, desperately. (He was lying, but he hoped he could talk her round, knowing that, underneath, she was simply a kid who had once gone to his school.)

'To stop people like you, Dylan ... people who TELL ME WHAT TO DO! And now that all the superheroes – and Iguana Boy – are out of the way—'

'Hey, that was unnecessary,' said Dylan, hurt.

'Now that you are all out of the way,' continued the Platypus Kid, ignoring him completely, 'I can carry out the next part of my plan. To rule every country, to take over the world, so that no one can tell me what to do ever again!'

There was a long pause.

'I understand your frustrations, I really do ...' began Dylan, desperately.

'You understand? You understand

nothing! Tell me, why would you want to be a superhero like this lot?' asked the Platypus Kid, moving closer to the prison cell. 'All they do is laugh at you and boss you around. I know what that's like. People have been telling me what to do ever since I can remember – but not any more.'

Suddenly, an idea flashed into Celina's mind and it had escaped her mouth before she had even really considered it. 'Why don't you join me?'

'What?' said Dylan, confused.

'Become a supervillain like me. Your family doesn't seem to want to know you – none of them respect you ... all because you can talk to an animal. Well, *I* respect that ...

I know what it's like. Become a supervillain, like me.'

'You can have him,' said Millie Monday.

'Yeah, he'll never be a real superhero,' added Arctic Thunder.

Dylan thought about what she was offering – the chance to help rule the world. Perhaps in time he could actually make the world a better place, make the Platypus Kid see the benefits of helping others and, slowly but surely, turn her into a superhero. But, deep down, he knew it was wrong and that the end didn't justify the means. He could *never* be a supervillain, not even for a single day.

'No!' he shouted. 'I will never join you!

You may have a similar power to me, but we are not the same. It's not the power you have that defines you, it's how you choose to use it that counts! I'm a hero, born to help others, and that is what I intend to do.'

'Very noble. Foolish, but noble.' The Platypus Kid smoothed down her mask. 'Mostly foolish, though. In fact, I take back the whole noble thing – it's just foolish. So be it. You can serve me along with everyone else.' The Platypus Kid turned and walked away.

The superheroes let out a collective groan.

'You FOOL!' shouted Terrifying Suzanne. 'You should have said, "Of course I'll join you." Then, when you were out of the cage, you could have knocked her on the head, and let us all out!' She slumped into a corner.

'It's a classic superhero trick – pretend to fight with your friends then, POW!' said Arctic Thunder. 'But then, what would you know about superhero tricks? You'll never be a superhero, little bro. You just don't have what it takes.'

Dylan stared down at his flippers. *Perhaps he's right. Maybe I don't have what it takes.* He rested his head on the bars, ready to admit defeat. That is, until he noticed something rather familiar on the table behind the Platypus Kid.

Surely they hadn't ...

He tapped on the bars and the Platypus Kid stopped. 'I heard what they said, Iguana Boy. Don't think I'm letting you out now.'

'I know, you would never fall for a classic superhero trick. But I do have a question for you.'

'And what might that be?' said the Platypus Kid, turning around.

'Do you like pizza?'

'Of course I like pizza. Everyone does.'

'What about that pizza over there?' Dylan pointed to the unopened pizza box he had noticed on the table.

'I haven't had a slice yet, although it smelt very nice. Come to think of it, I don't actually remember ordering a pizza ...'

THE REAL PLAN

PAUL: 'OK, SO AFTER DYLAN GETS KNOCKED OUT BY WHAT I ASSUME WILL BE A PLATYPUS HOLDING A CRICKET BAT, THE REAL PLAN KICKS INTO ACTION ...'

PAUL: 'AT THIS POINT, THE PLATYPUS KID WILL THINK SHE HAS NEUTRALISED THE THREAT. ANOTHER FANTASTIC VICTORY. AND WHAT BETTER WAY TO CELEBRATE THAN ...'

RED EYE: 'PIZZA!'

PAUL: 'EXACTLY. WE RING THE DOORBELL AND GET IN THE PIZZA BOX. THEN WE WAIT TO BE PICKED UP.'

SMELLY PAUL: 'WHAT DO WE DO TO PASS THE TIME WHILE WE'RE IN THERE?'

PAULINE: 'WE CAN PLAY I SPY.'

SMELLY PAUL: 'I SPY, WITH MY LITTLE EYE ...'

PAUL: 'IS IT 'BOX' AGAIN?'

SMELLY PAUL: 'HOW DID YOU KNOW?!?'

PAULINE: 'WE'RE INSIDE THE WAREHOUSE! NO ONE CAN RESIST FREE PIZZA! TIME FOR YOUR PLAN, PAUL!'

PAUL: 'OK! LET'S BREAK THOSE LAZY SUPERHEROES OUT!'

Over the course of human history, or more accurately superhero history, there have been some truly epic battles; but in the years that followed, many would agree there have been none more spectacular than Iguana Boy vs the Platypus Kid.

It was like watching an immovable object meet an unstoppable force. Or, more accurately, an extremely movable object meeting a pretty weak force. OK, it was more like watching iguanas fight platypuses but, nonetheless, it was spectacular. Spectacularly odd.

'Stop him!' shouted the Platypus Kid, as Smelly Paul ran towards the Superpower Neutraliser Machine.

The platypuses growled back. A group of them ran forward with their cricket bats and started whirling them around wildly. The iguanas slapped the platypuses in the face with their pizza slices, causing hot melted cheese to stick to their rather delicate fur. The platypuses tried to rub it off, but they ended up getting stuck to their own fur, falling to the floor in a tangled, tangy cheese knot.

Red-Eye, Paul and Pauline then flung themselves at the next wave of platypuses, grabbing their beaks and using their extra-strong grip to hold on for the ride. The platypuses then tried to hit the iguanas. Just before the bats connected, the iguanas let go and the platypuses ended up hitting each other on the head.

Another group chased after Smelly Paul who was whistling innocently as he made progress towards the Superpower Neutraliser Machine. As they got closer, they began to smell something terrible. They covered their big beaks with their webbed paws, but every step they took, the stench grew stronger.

When they had made it to a single step away from him, they fell to the floor.

'Grr!' they exclaimed, holding their beaks for dear life.

'What do you mean, "He stinks too much"?' shrieked the Platypus Kid.

'GRRRRR!'

'What do you mean you're not touching him?'

The Platypus Kid started to run towards Smelly Paul but it was too late. He was at the machine, right next to the 'Stop' button.

'Why, oh, why, did I write "Stop" on the button?' shouted the Platypus Kid.

(It's not known why supervillains feel the need to put a giant button on their machines that completely disable them, or why they feel the need to write the word 'Stop' in giant letters to give away said button's purpose. But they do. Every time ...)

With a smack of Smelly Paul's tail, the button was pressed and the Superhero Neutraliser Machine was turned off.

Seconds later, the lair turned into chaos and the battle truly began. A huge black cloud formed at the roof of the warehouse. Lightning bolts shot out of Arctic Thunder's finger tips, burning the platypuses on their bums, while Terrifying Suzanne looked angrily at them (which made a few of them cry).

'Stand back,' shouted Atomic Adam, lifting his shirt and collecting the fluff from his belly button. He threw it at the Superpower Neutraliser Machine and it exploded.

Millie Monday would have helped out, but it was Tuesday, so she didn't.

Lacey Shoestring retied everyone's shoelaces during the battle, like a pro, while Millie Monday shouted words of encouragement at her.

With the force field down and all of the superheroes free, the platypuses dropped their cricket bats and put their webbed paws over their heads in surrender (apart from the platypuses that had been hit by the pizza – their arms were still stuck fast with cheese).

The Platypus Kid quickly followed suit. It was over.

'It's over, Platypus Kid. You won't be ruling the world anytime soon,' said a triumphant Dylan.

'No thanks to you,' she replied. 'Although it seems I underestimated you, Iguana Boy. You and your ugly little lizards.'

'Ugly? Have you ever actually looked at one of your platypuses?'

'Hey, leave my platypuses alone.'

'You started it.'

'No, you started it by ruining my plan.'

'No, you started it by calling my iguanas ugly.'

'No, you started it.'

'No, you started it.'

This went on for some time. In fact, although there are no official records for the longest back and forth of the 'No, you started it' argument, if there were, this would almost certainly be in the top three.

Paul and his fellow iguanas looked on, realising that, at the end of the day, Dylan was just a kid. A kid who, with their help, had managed to save the world with a triple-cheese pizza.

After a few minutes, all the superheroes, platypuses and iguanas were huddled around the two of them as they continued their heated debate. The platypuses looked at the iguanas and although they couldn't speak each other's language, they seemed to understand each other.

They nodded in recognition and shouted, **'STOP IT!'** at the same time. To the majority of superheroes in the room, they simply heard a growl and a weird, lizard-like tongue click.

Iguana Boy and the Platypus Kid stopped. They looked around to see that everyone had gathered around them, and was staring. They felt a little embarrassed.

'OK, perhaps I did start it. Maybe if I didn't hate being told what to do so much we wouldn't be here right now,' admitted the Platypus Kid to everyone's amazement (including her own).

'That would have been nice,' said Dylan, putting a hand on her shoulder. 'And I bet that picture you drew at school of the zoo would have been really awesome with a lion in it, too.'

'NO, IT WOULDN'T! STOP TELLING ME WHAT TO DO WITH MY ZOO PICTURE!'

And, just like that, the Platypus Kid entered yet another raging temper she couldn't control.

'I would tell her to calm down,' Dylan said to his iguanas, 'but I don't think she would take too kindly to that. Take her away,' he added, waving a hand towards the exit, desperately trying to hide his smile. (He had always wanted to say, 'Take her away' about a supervillain after saving the world. Now that the time had come, he couldn't help but enjoy it.)

A rather large-looking superhero walked over, hoisted the Platypus Kid onto his shoulder and carried her towards the exit.

'I'll get you one day, Iguana Boy!' screamed the Platypus Kid, her voice reverberating as she left the warehouse.

But the empty threats from the Platypus Kid were soon drowned out by cheering from his fellow superheroes. That's right ... fellow superheroes – his peers, colleagues, working acquaintances ... Dylan could call them all these names, and more, for now he really was a real-life superhero.

But as much as he would have liked to take the credit, there was a group of very special iguanas Dylan had yet to thank. He approached his friends, who were sitting perched on the edge of the pizza box. Smelly Paul was rubbing a slice of pizza under his armpits.

'What are you doing?' asked Dylan.

'What? It smells better than I do.'

'Good point,' said Dylan, laughing. He gave Smelly Paul a pat on the head.

'It worked! Our plan actually worked!' said Red-Eye.

'Yeah ... about that' said Dylan. 'I take back what I said about the pizza plan, I was wrong. It was genius, Pauline.'

'Thank you, Iguana Boy,' said Pauline, doing a little curtsey with an imaginary dress.

'I owe you guys so much, thank you. You were incredible out there. Brave, strong, intelligent and fearsome – did I mention fearsome?'

'I think you mentioned fearsome,' said Paul.

Dylan couldn't remember ever being this happy. Looking around at his new friends he could honestly say he wouldn't swap his power for anything else. Not even the ability to fly or turn invisible. This was probably exactly how Metallic Kid had felt after defeating Veggie Boy.

However, there was one small issue that had yet to be explained to Dylan.

'One thing, though, guys,' said Dylan, crouching down to whisper so the other superheroes wouldn't hear him. (It was an unnecessary move, as the other superheroes weren't paying him any attention: they were too busy rewriting the story of what had happened, giving themselves more important roles in proceedings – Arctic Thunder, for example, had apparently planned the whole thing with Dylan, so had been captured on purpose ...)

'You hid in the pizza box, came in, waited for the perfect moment to spring your surprise and then you broke the superheroes out of the prison, forcing the Platypus Kid to surrender. It really was a great plan.'

'Thank you', said Pauline and Paul at the same time.

'What I don't understand is why we knocked on the door selling cookies.'

'That was my idea,' said Red-Eye, straightening his imaginary tie (which looked weird, as he didn't wear clothes).

'OK, great, so how did it fit into the overall plan?'

'Well, we needed to get rid of you as you wouldn't go for the whole pizza plan, which we all knew would totally work.'

'And you were right.' Dylan smiled at his

team. 'I wish you could have told me but I doubt I would have listened. Wait ... that still doesn't explain why I was dressed as a penguin.'

'I just thought it was funny,' said Red-Eye with a cheesy grin (a real cheesy grin – the iguanas had been tucking into the remaining pizza).

Dylan stared blankly at Red-Eye. In his defence, it was pretty funny.

All of the superheroes gathered around Dylan and the iguanas to get a closer look. One or two of them gave them a little pet on their backs. For Dylan's sake, the iguanas simply ignored it.

Atomic Adam approached, a beaming

smile stretching from ear to ear. 'Thank you, Iguana Boy. You saved the world – with a triple-cheese pizza, no less.'

'I was just doing my duty,' said Dylan, his cheeks getting ever so slightly red.

'Yes, it is your duty, because as far as I am concerned, you are one of us now. And I'm not the only one who thinks so, am I, Ron?'

'Indeed,' said a voice, which boomed around the warehouse. It was Ron Strongman, his voice amplified by a superhero who had the ability to turn his mouth into a very loud speaker system.

'I have heard of your triumph here today, Iguana Boy, and would like to formally invite you to join us at the Superhero Collective.'

'Wow ... I don't know what to say,' said Dylan, lost for words. 'Do I get a cape?'

Ron Strongman laughed (he clearly thought that was a joke. He hated superheroes who insisted on wearing capes. He had even written about it on a toilet wall at Superhero HQ). 'See you soon, Iguana Boy.'

Ron's voice disappeared and the superheroes began to leave. All who remained were Dylan, the iguanas and his brother and sister.

'We owe you an apology,' said Millie Monday, dragging Arctic Thunder over to their brother.

Arctic had a hard time apologising for anything, even when he was wrong, so

'Hrrrmph,' was all he said in agreement.

'We are sorry. Well done, little bro.'

At this moment, Paul climbed up Dylan's leg, perched on his shoulder and said in a low voice into his ear: 'Who does this guy think he is, huh? Oh, now he's Mr Nice Guy but ten minutes ago he was laughing at you!'

'At least he didn't dress me as a penguin,' said Dylan.

Arctic Thunder noticed Paul and smiled. 'Hello, Spartacus, good to see you again. Do you remember me?'

'If he comes any closer, I'm gonna bite his nose off!'

'Did he just say something? What did he say?'

Dylan paused for a second. 'He said he remembers you! How about a kiss?'

Arctic Thunder really should have known better than to lean in close to a superhero's iguana...

'OUCH!' he screamed, running out of the warehouse holding his nose, with Millie Monday frantically chasing after him.

Dylan and Paul shared a high five, as the other Pauls and Pauline all climbed up onto Dylan's shoulders.

'Don't forget the pizza!' shouted Paul, as they made their way towards the exit. Dylan turned around and grabbed the box. There was one slice left. He picked it up and gave it to Paul, who broke it into pieces to share it amongst his friends. (Dylan declined a bite, having realised just how long the iguanas must have been sitting on top of it whilst hiding in the box.)

'Shall we?' said Dylan, gesturing towards the exit.

'Lead the way,' said Paul, with a smile.

Dylan left the warehouse and was greeted by the most glorious sunny day he had ever seen. (Maybe it was, or maybe everything just felt a little brighter since he had saved the world.)

The iguanas chewed happily on their pizza and Dylan took a single step forward. A step towards the beautiful sunshine. A step towards being a real-life superhero. A step towards his next exciting adventure.

For the adventures of Iguana Boy had only just begun ...

APPROVED

SUPERHERO COLLECTIVE HQ ID PASS

NAME: DYLAN SPENCER

AKA: ~~BLIZZARD LIZARD~~ IGUANA BOY

SUPERPOWER: TALKING TO IGUANAS

AGE/HEIGHT: 9yrs/4ft 3ins

DISGUISE: CAPE!

FAVOURITE ANIMAL: ~~CATS~~ IGUANAS

FAVOURITE PIZZA TOPPING: TRIPLE CHEESE

ACKNOWLEDGEMENTS

THERE ARE FAR TOO MANY PEOPLE TO ACKNOWLEDGE SO LET ME BEGIN WITH A SWEEPING, ALL-ENCOMPASSING STATEMENT ...

THANK YOU.

THAT WAS FOR YOU (YES YOU!) IF YOU'RE READING THIS THEN I OWE YOU A TREMENDOUS AMOUNT OF THANKS, NO MATTER HOW WELL ACQUAINTED WE ARE. MORE DIRECTLY I MUST THANK MY WIFE FOR PUSHING ME (NOT PHYSICALLY) AND SUPPORTING ME AND MY SON ZAC UNCONDITIONALLY. MY SON'S CHEEKY SMILE IS ALL THE MOTIVATION I REALLY NEED.

TO MUM AND DAD FOR LETTING ME CARVE OUT MY PATH WITHOUT JUDGEMENT - AND FOR YOUR UNWAVERING BELIEF IN ME.

TO LORRAINE KELLY (I DIDN'T EXPECT TO BE WRITING THAT IN THE ACKNOWLEDGEMENTS OF MY FIRST BOOK), TOM FLETCHER FOR HIS KIND WORDS, AND EVERYONE ELSE INVOLVED IN TOP TALES, THE COMPETITION THAT BROUGHT THIS BOOK TO LIFE.

TO EVERYONE AT THREE WHO HAS SUPPORTED ME ON THIS JOURNEY, PROVIDING MUCH INSPIRATION (PIZZA WITH HOLES IN) ALONG THE WAY.

TO MY BEST FRIEND CHRIS, FOR ALL OF YOUR KNOWLEDGE ON THE BOOK INDUSTRY AND TO JIM, FOR HELPING ME TO RELAX WITH STORIES ABOUT THOSE BELOVED ARSENAL GLORY DAYS! OH, AND CHRIS DOUCH. DEEP PAN?

TO RIKIN PAREKH FOR MAKING THE PICTURES IN MY HEAD COME TO LIFE (BY NO MEANS AN EASY JOB ...) I COULDN'T BE HAPPIER WITH DYLAN AND HIS IGUANA PALS. TO MY AGENT EVE WHITE FOR TAKING ME ON AND SHOWING ME THE ROPES.

AND FINALLY TO EVERYONE AT HODDER CHILDREN'S WHO HAVE HELPED MAKE MY DREAMS COME TRUE, IN PARTICULAR TO POLLY LYALL GRANT AND ANNE MCNEIL, WHO HAVE BEEN WITH ME (AND DYLAN) THE WHOLE WAY AND HAVE HELPED ME BECOME A MUCH MORE STRUCTURED PERSON (MY WIFE THANKS YOU TOO).

AND TO LYNNE MANNING FOR THE BEAUTIFUL DESIGN.

THIS WOULDN'T HAVE HAPPENED WITHOUT ALL OF YOU.

PIZZA AND LOVE TO YOU ALL.